Book One in the War Faery Trilogy

Lush Publications

PERTH

Published in Perth, Australia by Lush Publications.
First Published in Australia 2014

Cover Design: Melody Simmons
Editor: Felicity Kay

Usher, Donna Joy
Faery Born
ISBN: 978-0-9873207-4-2
Pp290

Acknowledgements

I would like to take this opportunity to thank all of my loyal fans for your emails, tweets and Facebook messages. Your kind words make the late nights and hard work worth it.

Thanks also go to my editor, Felicity Kay, for her tireless work, her in-depth grammar lessons and her sparkling company, and to my cover designer, Derek Murphy, for another amazing cover.

Last but not least, I would like to thank you for buying *Faery Born*. I truly hope you enjoy it.

Wind rushed past my face as Emerald dipped a wing and swung back towards the battle. Goblins and Border Guards fought amongst the trees, the superior-numbered goblins forcing the Guard back towards the castle.

As one, Emerald and I screamed our defiance; lightning flashed from my fingertips and fire roared from her breath. Crossbow bolts bounced off her hide as we raced to engage them.

Indomitable Emerald, glorious and powerful. Her giant heart thundered beneath me as she hurtled us through the sky.

I thought nothing could stop her, but the tip of a bolt sliced through her wing's membrane. She screeched in rage as we pivoted to the side and plummeted towards the earth.

I wrapped my arms around her neck, pressing my face to her scales as we smashed into the trees. Wood tore and shrieked around us as we tumbled, finally crashing to a halt against the trunk of a large oak.

Emerald's mind touched mine for the briefest of moments.

Fight, little one. Fight.

Sword held high, I turned to face the goblin warriors as they stepped from the trees.

Chapter One

Be Careful What You Wish For

Willing my eyelids to stay open, I stared at the page. It wasn't that I didn't find the history of the Dark Years interesting, it was the fact that I had been studying for days.

Jumping to my feet, I shook my head and waved my arms around. Only one more day and then the final exams would be over. I couldn't believe it. Almost finished school.

Reminding myself that I wouldn't be finishing anything if I didn't pass this exam, I picked the book up and carried it with me while I walked.

The Dark Years. I had only been five when they had ended, but the chaotic fear that had ruled during that time had seeped deep into my pores. Reading about it, thinking about it, made me sick to my core.

Santanas Gabrielle (the name sent a shiver down my spine no matter how many times I heard it), had been the last living War Faery. Before him, War Faeries had been benefactors of the people. They'd used their incredible powers to serve and protect. But before him, none had ever gone mad.

A mad War Faery, hell bent on raising his wife from the dead.

Santanas had done evil, unspeakable things.

Oh, they had fought him. They had fought the goblins that had ransacked the land in his name; no city left untouched, no village left whole. They had fought to save the children being sacrificed in his black-magic attempts to re-gain his love. And they had been partly successful. But enough children had disappeared from their beds, their broken bodies discovered deep in the woods, to leave a lasting impression.

Wards he'd placed on his body meant they hadn't been able to kill him. So they'd trapped him. Tricked by a lover, he'd drunk a potion that had torn his spirit from his body and entombed it in a rock. The rock had disappeared soon after, but that hadn't dampened the jubilation in the streets.

They said nobody could fracture his soul from that stone, that the spell they had used to entomb him couldn't be broken. They said he could never rise again. But history had showed that *never* sometimes *could.*

A terrified child clawed her way to the front of my mind, stealing my breath and freezing my blood.

What if? What if he were to rise again?

I slammed the book shut and took a deep breath. I wasn't a small child hiding under her bed any more. I was seventeen for goodness' sake, soon to be eighteen.

That thought distracted me more than any other could have. I sighed and thumped the textbook back onto the table.

On their seventeenth birthdays all witches received a wand. Some time between then, and when they turned eighteen, their 'familiars' found them. Until then, witches didn't have access to their powers. I would be eighteen in nine days. Only nine days for my familiar to find me or they never would.

I pulled my wand out of my hair (its only current use was as a hair pin) and flicked it at the text book. 'Risius textbook.'

Nothing happened.

I kicked one of the chairs before pulling it out and slumping into it. Only nine more days.

'Isadora Scrumpleton.' My mother was standing in the door to the kitchen.

'What?' I replied. The look on my mother's face hardened. 'Sorry,' I added.

Her familial, tabby cat, Sebastian, stuck his head between her legs and stared at me with large, topaz eyes.

This just in, Goblins have attacked Little Downs.

We both turned to stare at the television. Mum picked up the remote and increased the volume. The screen showed buildings in flames with smoke pouring out of them. A group of witches worked together to contain the fire. One human held a hose; its ineffective flow doing nothing more than making him feel helpful.

The full extent of the damage is not yet known, but several people have been hospitalised and a few are reported missing.

A woman staggered into view. 'Donald,' she screamed. 'Donald.' Blood trickled from a wound on her scalp.

I put my hands over my mouth as I stared at the macabre scene.

Mum flicked off the television. 'That's the third attack this week.'

'How far away is Little Downs?'

'A few hundred miles north west. A long way away.'

'They're getting closer.'

She moved over to me and smoothed my hair back from my face. 'We're too close to London for them to dare attack us.'

I wasn't so sure; fear crept up my spine.

'What's got into you?' she asked.

I rolled my eyes at the television. Like goblin raids weren't enough to be worried about.

'That's not what had you in a froth before.'

I sighed. 'The final exam is tomorrow.'

'Do you need help studying?'

'It's not the theory. It's the practical.'

'You know the prac isn't marked.'

'It's so humiliating, standing in front of the class waving my wand.' I crossed my arms over my chest and stuck out my bottom lip. 'I may as well be waving a chopstick.'

'Yes, well, there have been cases of a familiar choosing a witch without the witch realising. Remember Lara Huntley's grandson? He was chosen by a bumblebee. They would never have realised, if not for the practical tests.'

Mum,' I paused for a second, almost too scared to voice my real concern, 'what if I don't get chosen?'

'You will darling.'

'I'm nearly eighteen. What if I don't? There was that kid over at Dartsmouth College that never got chosen.'

'I hear he has a very good job at a law firm in London.'

'I don't want to work at a law firm.' I resisted the urge to stomp my feet.

'What do you want to do?'

The question stumped me. I had been so focused on my powers coming in that I hadn't thought beyond that. 'I don't know.'

'Well maybe you should concern yourself with that.' She ran her hands over her strawberry-blonde hair, tucking the bits that had escaped her bun behind her ears. 'Now I need to work on a potion for The Weekly Witching News and you need to study.' She disappeared back into the kitchen, leaving me staring at my books and wondering what I wanted to do with the rest of my life.

***

The students' chatter in the Eynsford College courtyard was a low rumble. I could hear the occasional mutter about goblins, but most of the conversations were centred on exams and holidays.

I buried my head in my textbook and pretended to be unaware of what was going on around me. I always found that was the best way to escape the attention of the school bullies. Until Sabina got there with her wand, I was easy prey.

'Still studying?' Sabby threw her bag onto a seat and then gracefully sat beside me. The sun caught in her fiery-red hair and lit her green eyes.

'Trying to forget about the stupid prac.'

'Oh Izzy,' she said, shaking her head. 'I don't know why you get so worked up about it, nobody else cares.'

'It's easy for you to say.' I looked down to where her huge, black cat sat at her feet. Phantom had showed up the very afternoon of her seventeenth birthday.

'You'll get chosen. You're a pedigree, pure-blooded witch.'

The bell rang. I sighed and closed the textbook. Hopping up, I scanned the courtyard for Isgranelda and her gang. The last thing I needed on my way to the exam was to be 'accidentally' tripped.

I claimed a seat near the back of the exam hall and took some calming breaths while I waited for the start bell to ring. When it did, I pushed all thoughts of the practical from my mind and turned over the exam paper.

I read through the questions, relaxing as I did. No nasty surprises. An essay on the Great Faery War, discussing how it had shaped the Magic Conventions that governed us today; and one on the cultural initiation of the War and the steps taken to ensure such a travesty wouldn't occur again. The last question was on the Dark Years.

Santanas Gabrielle. I'd heard people muttering that he would rise again. Admittedly, this muttering had been done after a drink or two at the Toasted Toadstool, where I waited on tables, and was normally shouted down quite quickly. But lately, with the goblin attacks becoming more frequent, the muttering had become louder and the shouting down not quite so quick.

I finished the exam with quarter of an hour to go. I could see Sabby staring into space while she chewed the end of her pencil. She had been hand-selected in the Academy of Advanced Witching's early academy trials and offered a scholarship. Her magical strength lay in healing. She could already force tissue to knit back together and bones to straighten. That was what made her a formidable ally. While she chose to use her talents for good, the truth was, she could also inflict pain.

Finally, the bell indicating the end of the exam rang, causing everyone but me to cheer. We waited while the papers were collected and then there was a stampede of humans departing the building.

'Right,' said Radismus Prangle, the head of the Magic Department, 'who wants to go first?'

Several hands shot up in the air. I was surprised to see Sally Blumberry's was amongst them. 'Must want to get the torture over early,' I whispered as I nodded towards Sally.

'Oh, didn't you know?'

'Know what?' My voice sounded sickly even to *my* ears.

'She got chosen yesterday.'

As if on cue, Sally hopped up and strode to the front of the room. A shiny, black raven perched on her shoulder, peeping out from under her thick, curly hair.

She waved her wand at a chair, which rose obediently into the air. A polite smatter of applause followed her successful levitation. I felt a cold sweat break out on the back of my neck.

'She's a natural,' said Sabina. 'It took me weeks to levitate a chair after I was chosen.'

Unlike the faeries, who worked with the five elements, witches' powers were target orientated. More like talent. My Mum's strength lay in household needs. She could use her magic for any household chore. That's why her column on The Weekly Witching News was so popular. She designed potions to do what *she* could with the flick of her wand, and then other witches could also use magic to clean and cook.

Some witches were inventors, some builders, some farmers and hunters. The different ways the power presented were varied, every witch's powers uniquely their own. The trick was finding the extent of a witch's capabilities.

I could hear Radismus congratulating Sally and giving her instructions on what spells he wanted her to try. His job was to work out where our magical talents lay.

'Oh well that still leaves Leonard, Beryl and Anthea,' I said.

'Hmmm,' Sabina responded.

'Hmmmm?' I replied.

'Well, I overheard Leonard and Beryl swapping stories this morning. Turns out they've both been picked.'

'Whizbang.' I shot a panicked look at Anthea who was sitting on the far side of the room. She glanced over at me, her thick glasses making her eyes look enormous. Her face took on a sympathetic look as she lifted the arm of the cardigan slung over her shoulders. A snake, disturbed from its warm bower, lifted its head and flicked its tongue while it tasted the air, searching for danger.

I groaned and sat back in my seat. I couldn't believe it. I was the only one. The last. I could feel the icy fingers of fear clutching at me.

What if I didn't get chosen? What if I were forever cut off from my powers?

Tears threatened as I watched my classmates perform the spells set for them by Radismus. And then, it was my turn. I could feel curious eyes boring into my back as I walked to the front.

'Lucky last Isadora,' Radismus boomed. I wished he would keep his voice down; I wasn't feeling so lucky. 'Let's see if you can levitate that chair.'

'I can't,' I told him.

'You don't know unless you try,' he responded much too cheerfully. 'Remember Ralph Huntley?'

'Yes, I know. He was chosen by a bumblebee and they never would have known if he hadn't tried.' I had my doubts about that story. I mean, how could you not notice a bumblebee harassing you?

As I lifted my wand I noticed Isgranelda nudge Gretchen. They were sitting in the front row.

Oh Great.

'Risius chairius,' I squeaked. Not surprisingly, nothing happened.

'Why don't you give it another go?' Radismus's voice was filled with empathy. 'This time, say it like you mean it.'

I could hear the front row girls giggling. 'Maybe her wand's broken.' Isgranelda's thick accent made the words sound broken and clipped.

I squirmed as my face started to burn.

'Oh look, her face is on fire,' Gretchen said.

I could see Sabby's sympathetic face near the back, but the rest of the students broke into laughter. It rippled across the hall to where I stood sweating.

I lifted my wand and concentrated on the chair.

'Visualise the chair lifting into the air,' Radismus crooned, 'see it floating.'

A spit ball smacked into my forehead. It quivered there for a second before falling to the floor where it lay in a goopy mess. I could hear sniggering as I wiped at my forehead with the back of my arm. Another one quickly followed the first. This one entangled itself into the hair hanging to the side of my face. I had to give it to Aphrode - she was a great shot.

'Lift your arm and command the chair.'

I mean seriously, could he not *see* the incoming spit balls?

I looked out over the hall to Sabby. Anger blazed across her face and danced in her eyes. Her face was grim as she mouthed, 'You can do it.' No-one *ever* teased Sabina.

As I met her eyes, her fury infected me. How dare they make fun of me?

'Isadora is a witch or so we think.' The girls started the chant, but it quickly spread through the room, flowing up to mock me.

A pressure built inside me, stretching me like a balloon. It filled me up, threatening to burst from my pores and roar towards the girls in the front row.

The next spit ball narrowly missed my eye. I could feel myself losing control; the strange power licking out towards them. I strained to hold it back. But each peal of laughter weakened my restraint until finally, like a wave, it broke over my boundaries and roared towards them. I pointed my wand at them and shrieked, 'Risius chairius.'

Every chair in the hall shot into the air. The previously giggling students squealed with terror. I held my wand up as the power washed through me and rolled out into the room.

'Isadora.' I could hear Radismus calling my name.

'Help me,' I said from between clenched teeth. My arm was shaking with the exertion of controlling the power.

'Very gently,' he said in a calm voice, 'lower your wand.'

I lowered my arm a few inches and the chairs plummeted a foot towards the floor. Several students screamed in terror.

'Carefully,' said Radismus.

As slowly as I could, I moved my wand towards the ground. I could hear some sobbing coming from the front row and I was trying not to feel pleased, but after the years of torment it was hard not to.

Here was the weird thing though - while Gretchen clung to the back of her chair with both arms, and Aphrode stared at the ground while she wailed, Isgranelda sat straight in her chair and stared at me, a triumphant look on her face.

'I think I'll drop around sometime next week for a coffee,' Radismus said once the chairs were safely grounded. 'It's been ages since I've seen Prunella. Hopefully she'll make her famous lemon cake.'

'Okay.' I was confused. I had just levitated an entire room full of students, without a familiar, and he was more interested in my mother's lemon cake. It was all a bit weird.

Radismus clapped his hands. 'Class dismissed,' he decreed. 'Have a great holiday, and good luck with the rest of your lives.'

Everyone, except Sabina, sprinted from the hall. I could hear their cheering and yelling and I wished I could join in their merriment.

'Holy moley,' Sabby said, staring at me with wide eyes. 'That was amazing. Why didn't you tell me you had a familiar?'

'I don't.'

'You just levitated a room full of people.'

'Seriously Sabby, I *haven't.*'

'So it's an embarrassing animal. What is it? A slug?'

'No.'

'An ant?'

'I don't…'

'Ooh. Don't tell me - it's a *spider.*'

I stopped and grabbed her by the shoulders. 'Sabby, I haven't been chosen.'

She looked up at me for a few seconds and then burst out laughing. 'Of course you have. Come on let's go home and get ready for tonight. We've got some celebrating to do.' She grabbed my hand and dragged me off towards the car park while she chatted excitedly about what she was going to wear that night.

I tried to listen to her, but I couldn't forget the feel of the power coursing through me. I had had many discussions with Mum and Grams about how it felt to cast a spell, and it had never sounded like that. A burst of energy, a moment where you felt yourself expanding beyond, a second of inexplicable power, a flash of lightning, but never a raging torrent that stretched to the horizon of your mind.

I was scared and confused, but mainly I was relieved. It appeared I was *not* going to have to get a good job at a law firm in London, and to me, at that moment, *that* was the most important thing.

Chapter Two

You Call *That* A Familiar?

I went for a run when I got home; partly because I hadn't exercised for days, but mostly because I didn't want to answer any questions about the exam. I knew I'd have to talk about it eventually, but for the moment I wanted to be alone to think.

The feel of the pavement passing beneath my feet was hypnotic, and after I had run a couple of miles I felt myself starting to relax. Maybe I *had* been chosen. Maybe the whole bumblebee thing wasn't so far off the mark. But there was a huge amount of prestige surrounding the type of familiar that chose you, and I had been hoping for an impressive one. I was going to be disappointed if it were a nit.

Cats were the most popular. Especially cats like Phantom: huge, aggressive and aloof. After that it was the reptiles. Diamond pythons topped the chart with the smaller, venomous varieties not too far behind. Next on the list were the birds. Although it was cool to have a raven or a crow, budgies and cockatiels were not so desirable. Then there were the rats, which were better than mice, but even mice were better than insects. If you had to have a creepy-crawly the coolest were the arachnids, and I wasn't sure how I felt about sharing the rest of my life with a spider.

I ran past a field where a group of people were playing cricket. A batter hit the ball towards the boundary and a witch leapt into the air, far higher than was humanly possible, and hovered there, waiting to catch the ball.

'Impressive,' I muttered. Levitation of objects was common to all witches. Levitation of oneself was a great deal harder; something to do with equal and opposite forces.

Humans loved to think that while they slept, we all rode around on broomsticks. Apart from the fact that it was magically impossible, I had never worked out what their fascination with broomsticks was. How comfortable would it be to sit on a stick? Better a flying couch.

Their control over air meant that some faeries could create floating objects, but these were pulled by flying creatures and were rare.

I reached the pole I used to mark the halfway point of my run. A small, white dog sat next to it, his tongue hanging out as he smiled a wolfy grin.

'Hey boy.' I bent down to scratch his head and noticed my shoelace was undone. Lucky. Considering the day I was having I probably would have tripped on it and broken an arm.

I was re-tying it when I felt something warm and wet dribbling down the back of my right leg. Swinging around, I spied the dog with his leg still cocked.

'Bugger off.' I shoo-ed my hands at him.

He slumped to one side as he stared at me, and then he broke eye contact and proceeded to lick his balls.

'Charming.' I shook my head and started off towards home.

It wasn't till I got home that I realised the dog was still with me. He collapsed on the front door mat, panting and puffing.

I checked him over for a tag, but there was nothing on his black, studded collar. *Great.* I was going to have to find his owner without any help at all.

'Eric,' I said to the front door, 'it's Izzy.'

The house shuddered and then the front door swung open. Generations of Scrumpletons had lived here, breathing life and magic into their home. The result was a 'witching house'; a sentient being that protected us. The little dog leapt up and raced inside, making a beeline for the kitchen.

I patted the door frame as I entered and felt a glow through the palm of my hand. Eric was happy I was home.

'What's this?' Mum asked as the dog plonked himself in the middle of the room and started whining.

'A dog,' I replied.

'I can see that. Where did it come from?'

'He followed me home,' I said. 'Must be lost.' He walked over to where Mum was cutting up meat for dinner, and stood on his hind legs. 'And hungry,' I added.

'Poor fellow,' Mum said as she tossed him a piece of steak. Mum's familiar, Sebastian, jumped off the table where he had been sunning himself and sauntered into the kitchen to examine the new arrival. He extended his nose towards the dog and sniffed him. When he was satisfied there was no immediate threat, he turned his attention to Mum and miaowed.

'Oh all right,' Mum said, throwing a piece to him as well.

'Where's Grams?' I took a seat at the kitchen table.

'In her rooms.'

As if on cue, I heard footsteps echoing down the hall and Grandma Bella burst into the loungeroom. She wore a flouncy evening dress with her enormous python, Cyril, coiled around her shoulders like a shawl. Her hair, which had turned a shocking shade of pink since I'd last seen her, was piled on top of her head.

The photos of Grams on the sideboard show a young woman with movie-star looks and a large smile. The movie-star looks are faded but still present, as is the large, dimply smile and her mischievous, blue eyes.

'Wow,' I said. 'Got a date?'

'Oh yes, but that's not important. Sabby told me the good news.' She spied the dirty, white creature begging for food and her eyes widened in surprise. 'A dog?'

'Yes it's a dog,' I replied.

'There's no such thing as a dog.'

I looked at her in concern. 'Are you all right Grams?'

'What have I done?' She clutched her chest and sank into the chair opposite me, staring at me with wide eyes. 'How do you feel?'

'Fine, why?'

'It must be such a shock.'

'What are you talking about?' Even for Grams this was strange behaviour.

Mum stopped cutting and looked at Grams. 'You don't think?' She gestured at the dog.

'What else could it be?' Grams replied.

'Can someone please tell me what's going on?' I looked from Mum to Grams and back again.

'Izzy, where did you find this animal?' Mum asked.

'I was out running. He peed on my leg.'

'Dear me.' Mum slumped against the kitchen cabinetry. *'A dog?* I've never heard of such a thing.'

And then I finally twigged.

'Noooooooooo. No way. Absolutely not. You don't think…' I pointed at the dog, whom had begun to clean his private parts again. 'You don't think that *that* is my *familiar*?' I finished in a weak voice.

The look on Mum's face was sympathetic.

'Great Dark Sky.' I clutched my nose as a foul smell wafted over us. 'What *is* that?'

'I think your familiar just farted.' As Grandma Bella put her hands over her face, the front doorbell rang. 'That will be Lionel.' She jumped up and raced to the front door. 'Eric,' she called, 'you can let him in.'

'Who's Lionel?' I asked Mum as I stared at the dog.

'Lionel Heartfelt.'

'*The* Lionel Heartfelt?' Grams was dating the warlock famed for his dangerous exploratory forays into lands occupied by non-friendly magical beings?

I could hear Grams giggling at the front door. 'Oh Lionel,' she tittered, 'you shouldn't have. But I'm glad you did.' I wasn't sure how a 65-year-old woman could get her voice to sound so naughty.

She swished into the kitchen with a huge bunch of orange and yellow striped flowers that she placed on the table while she dug through a cupboard for a vase. The bunch of flowers crawled towards me, a large seedpod opening to expose row-after-row of sharp teeth.

'Whizbang.' I jumped from my seat as the pod snapped at my hand.

'Good move young lady,' Lionel boomed in his deep voice. 'I cultivated them from seeds I gathered in the Pixie Lands. Many a young pixie has lost its life playing hide-and-seek in the garden where these beauties grow.'

'Ohh,' I said, 'that's, umm, really nice of you to give some to Grandma Bella.'

'Lionel,' said Grams, 'this is my granddaughter Isadora, and my daughter Prunella.'

I was surprised to note that Mum turned a deep shade of red as he kissed her hand. I supposed he was rather dashing with the one white streak through his jet-black hair.

Lionel looked down and said, 'And who is this?'

I was horrified to see the dog lifting a leg to sprinkle on Lionel's shoe. I managed to stop him just in time. 'So sorry,' I garbled, 'it's a stray I found on the street.' I was not yet ready to admit that *this* was my familiar, *especially* not when he had just tried to mark the most prestigious warlock bachelor in the country's leg.

'Your beauty is complemented by a good heart.'

'Oh, gee thanks.' I was embarrassed to feel myself blushing.

'We had better go. We don't want to be late.' Grams looked quite chuffed with the effect her beau had had on us. 'Lionel is taking me to see the Mermaid Opera. Apparently it's wonderful.'

'It certainly is my dear, and we shan't be late. I have brought the floating chariot.'

'Oh Lionel,' Grams giggled, 'you shouldn't have.'

Mum and I trooped out the front on the pretence of waving them off. I know I, however, was keen to see the chariot.

Four white, winged horses, attached to a floating, golden chariot, hovered over our front lawn. The horses flapped their wings lazily as they waited for Grams and Lionel to climb the thin ladder that descended from the carriage to the ground. Once they were safely secured in the back, Lionel picked up the reins, clucked his tongue, and the horses changed their wing movement to a backward thrusting stroke that saw them leaping forwards through the sky. Grams let out a shriek of delight as the chariot raced from our yard.

Mum and I returned to the kitchen with the little dog trotting at my heels.

'Well Izzy,' Mum said, taking off her apron and hanging it up, 'I guess you had better start guessing his name.'

'We don't know *for sure* that he's my familiar.'

'Try a spell.'

I picked up my wand and waved it at my textbook. 'Comius textbookius.' The book flew off the table and thumped into my chest, knocking me off my feet and onto the floor.

Mum's blue eyes widened and her eyebrows shot up her forehead.

'Could have been a fluke,' I advised her as I clambered back to my feet. Waving my wand at a diningroom chair I said, 'Risius chairius.' The chair flung itself into the air, crashing into the ceiling with such force it wedged between two beams.

'Satisfied?' Mum stared at the hole in dismay.

'Sorry,' I said, grimacing.

'You go off with your…,' she looked down at him and shook her head, *'familiar,* and I'll deal with this.'

'Come on,' I said to the dog, gesturing towards the stairs to my room. He stayed where he was, lying on the kitchen floor. I nudged him with my toe and he rolled onto his back and waved his legs in the air. Sighing, I bent over and wrapped my arms around his middle, heaving him into the air. He squirmed and let out a long, wavering fart.

'Seriously? I said to Mum. 'What did I do to deserve this?'

'You always were a different child.'

Once we were both comfortable on my bed I started with the obvious names.

'Fido... Max… Fang.' I gauged his reaction as I said each one. Witches don't have full access to their powers until they complete the bond by guessing their familiar's name. If they fail to guess, the familiar will eventually depart, leaving them with only a fraction of the powers they would have had. The same as if a familiar died.

An hour later I was sitting on the edge of my bed staring into his brown eyes. 'You're sure it's not Fido?' I asked him.

He blinked but stayed exactly where he was.

'You're pretty cute.' I ruffled his coat. 'But you're a little dirty. We'll have to do something about that. I think I'll give you a bath before I take you out in public so you're not so scruffy.'

He leapt onto my lap and started licking my face.

'Euuuwww, your breath stinks.' I held him at arm's length. 'Scruffy?'

He barked in response and wagged his stubby tail.

'All right Scruffy,' I said in relief, 'how'd you like to meet my friend Sabby?'

'Ruuuf,' he said in response. I took that to be a yes.

I jumped in the shower and, as an afterthought, dragged Scruffy in with me. He didn't seem very impressed by the whole washing thing.

I towel-dried him and then turned to the difficult prospect of getting myself ready for the evening. Sabby and I were meeting at the Puffin' Dragon, a new bar in town.

I viewed my tall, skinny frame in the mirror. I didn't have much feminine shape, not having gotten either Mum or Gram's curves. In fact the only things I *had* gotten from them were my blue eyes.

In the end I put on a little, black dress and pulled on some crème pumps, teaming them with a matching clutch Grams had given me for my last birthday. I piled my long, dark hair on top of my head, letting some loose bits dangle down around my face, and placed some silver earrings in my lobes.

'Not bad,' I told my reflection. Scruffy seemed to approve. He looked up from his grooming and ruffed at me when I exited the bathroom.

'Come on, let's get you some dinner,' I told him. He certainly approved of that and raced off to the kitchen. I could hear him barking at Mum.

'You got it?' she asked me.

'Ahuh.' I nodded my head. 'It's Scruffy.'

'Figures.' She looked down at him. 'You're going to have to give him a bath.'

'I just did.'

'You wouldn't know.'

I looked at him. She was right. He appeared to be as dirty as before I had washed him. 'He looked clean when I'd finished. I'll get him some pet shampoo tomorrow.' I opened the fridge door and stared into its depths. What can we feed him?'

'I fed him while you were getting ready.'

'Really?' I had thought he had been lying in the doorway to my bedroom the whole time.

'He ate half a chicken.'

'Must have snuck out while I was doing my hair.'

'Which looks lovely by the way. Are you off now?'

'Yep. Off to be publicly humiliated.'

'Don't look at it like that.'

'Mum, I'm seventeen. Of course I'm going to look at it like that.'

Mum burst out laughing and hugged me. 'Well I'm proud of you,' she informed me. 'Now go have some fun.'

'Yes Ma'am.' I blew her a kiss and, with my familiar at my side, headed out the front door and into the night.

***

'A dog?' Sabina asked me for the fifth time.

'You're not going to stop are you?'

'I haven't been this shocked since Wally Wangleton pulled his pants down and showed us his privates.'

'Yes, well, we were *all* pretty speechless after that.' I paused and looked around the room. Already a few other students from Eynsford College had drifted in. 'What's wrong with a dog?'

I knew exactly what was wrong with a dog, but had convinced myself on the way to the Puffin' Dragon that if I owned the whole my-familiar-is-a-dog thing, that everyone else would accept it too. It was bad enough that most of the pub's patrons kept shooting sneaky glances at Scruffy. The fact that my best friend was having issues with it did not bode well.

'It's just not done.'

'Will you leave it alone.'

Picking up on my mood, she shut up about the dog thing and settled back into her chair. 'There's something different about you,' she finally said.

'I did my hair.'

'Not that.'

'I have make-up on.'

'Nope.'

'New dress?'

'Seen it.' She stared at me intently.

Scruffy, who had been off sniffing table legs and couches, sauntered back and jumped onto my lap. Phantom hissed and bared his teeth.

'Ahuh,' said Sabby. 'You're happy.'

'I'm always happy.'

'You're normally stressed, or worried, or nervous.'

'Yes, well, now I have Scruffy. I don't need to worry any more.'

'What? So that's it? All your troubles are over?'

'Ahuh,' I said.

'Without even going into the whole dog thing…,' I shot her a warning glance, and she stuck her tongue out before continuing, 'where are you going to college? What are you going to study? What do you want to do with your life?'

'Can't you just let me be happy?'

'Sorry.' She slouched back on the couch and sucked on a piece of her curly, red hair. 'It's just unnatural.'

'Me being happy is unnatural?'

'No, you *not* being worried about something is. It makes me nervous.'

We paused while our drinks were delivered to the table. I took a sip of mine and looked over at Sabby. She was drinking a dark, brown cocktail.

'What's that?' I asked.

'Troll Juice.'

'Sounds gross.'

'It's delicious,' she said. 'Want some?'

'No thanks. I'll stick to my Faery Water.'

The bar was beginning to fill up, most of the seats taken by students celebrating the end of school. A faint buzz of conversation could be heard over the music.

'What are you going to do now?' Sabina asked.

'You're not going to leave this alone are you?'

The front door of the bar slammed and the conversation buzz died down. Isgranelda pushed through the crowd to the bar, carrying Gretchen and Aphrode in her wake. Isgranelda was as tall and muscly as the other two were short and willowy. Anyone who protested at her pushing in was met with a stare filled with such vehemence that their protestations were wiped clear out of their head. She was one scary witch.

I slipped lower into my chair, hoping they wouldn't notice us.

'Of course you need to find out where your talent lies,' Sabina continued, seemingly oblivious to Isgranelda's entry.

I found myself wishing that invisibility was within the scope of a witch's talents. Now would be a good time to be invisible.

'And then think about what occupations fit into that talent.'

I could hear movement coming in our direction. Oh *please* don't let them see me.

'And then you need to…' She paused and looked over my shoulder, her face hardening at what she saw. 'You got a problem?' she asked.

'You're in our seats.' I didn't even need to look to know who was talking. I'd recognise Isgranelda's guttural accent anywhere.

Sabby's face took on a comical expression. 'Really? These seats are yours? Did someone steal them from your house?'

I loved Sabina with my whole heart, but sometimes I wished she weren't so brave. Either that, or that I was as brave as she was. It's hard to be brave though when you know someone can tie you up in knots with a flick of her wand.

'You've got a smart mouth,' Isgranelda growled.

'I've got a smart everything,' Sabby replied.

As if on its own, Sabina's Troll Juice floated into the air to hover over her.

'Don't you dare,' she gasped, trying to grab it.

The glass darted to the side and tipped so that the brown muck flowed over her head and down her black, silk dress. Pushing her wet hair out of her face, she glared at Isgranelda with fierce, green eyes. She flicked her wand towards the other woman so quickly I would have missed the movement if I hadn't been expecting it.

A whip cracked and Isgranelda grunted. 'You little bitch,' she hissed.

Without even thinking, I turned towards her. 'Don't call her that.'

'What are you going to do about it?'

Very good question. What was I going to do about it? What I would normally have done was slipped quietly out of the pub, but tonight I didn't feel like doing that. Tonight my blood boiled and beat within my vessels and I wanted some payback.

I stood and turned to face her. I was easily as tall as she was and I met her glare with all my anger. I had hoped that would have been enough to dissuade her from bullying us, but she was as mean as she looked.

She arched an eyebrow and suddenly my left arm was twisted painfully behind my back. I gasped and rose up on my tiptoes, trying to relieve the pressure. Scruffy let out a growl and leapt off his seat.

I heard a whip crack again and Isgranelda jerked in pain. A thin line of blood appeared on her cheek.

'Next time it will be your eyes.' Sabina's voice was cold and hard.

My arm released and Isgranelda took a step back. She looked at me for a long second and then said, 'Till tomorrow.'

I waited until the three of them had left the pub before sinking back onto my chair. My hands were shaking and my knees felt weak. What had gotten into me?

'Well,' Sabby pushed back her slimy hair, 'that went well.'

'No thanks to me,' I said.

'What do you think she meant?'

I had no idea, but Isgranelda's 'till tomorrow' had sent a chill down my spine. I had thought I was done with them now that school had finished.

'I need a shower.' Sabby grabbed her bag and stood up.

'You may need two.' I followed her to the front door of the pub, hoping Isgranelda had already cleared the area. There was no sign of them as we made our way to Sabby's car.

I waited while she rummaged through the boot, finally pulling out a plastic-backed picnic blanket. She spread it on the driver's seat before she hopped in. 'What are you doing tomorrow?' she asked me.

'Shopping, then fencing.' I pulled a face. I hated spending time in the shopping centre but I really had to get some things for Scruffy. Namely, shampoo. Plus, I still didn't have a dress for my party.

'Phooey,' Sabby said. 'I promised Mum I'd help her at work tomorrow.' Sabby made up for my lack of shopping enthusiasm tenfold.

We were silent for the rest of the drive home, and I was pleased when I found both Mum and Grams were out. I didn't feel like talking - not about the evening or my plans for life. All I felt like doing was hopping into bed and forgetting about the world for a while.

Chapter Three

En Garde

Things had not gone well at the pet store; a combination of the assistant not believing Scruffy was my familiar and me trying to prove I was a witch. I'd had to enlist the aid of another witch to get a bag of dog food off the ceiling.

In the end I'd grabbed a fire-engine-red collar, some shampoo, a bed, and a bag of dog food, without stopping to compare products or prices.

The shopping spree had gone downhill from there. *I* knew that I was too tall, too thin and had no boobs to speak of. I didn't need it being continuously pointed out to me by clothes designers and shop assistants. With only seven days to go to my party I had come home empty-handed.

No-one was home when I got back. Mum was in at the Weekly Witching News submitting a column on ridding your house of spiders, and goodness knows where Grams was. Probably down at the Toasted Toadstool Lodge regaling her friends with details of the naughtier parts of last night's date with Sir Lionel Heartfelt. That reminded me that I had to go to work after fencing and I raced up to my room to grab my uniform.

Sabby's face was floating in my bedroom mirror when I entered. Dubiously, I pulled my wand out of my hair and approached it; I'd never attempted reflective surface communications before. It wasn't a difficult spell, but it allowed you to talk over long distances. You could project yourself into any reflective surface at your desired destination but could not see anything until the spell was activated.

I pointed my wand at the mirror and said, 'Speakius clearius.' Her face, which had been lifeless, immediately became animated.

'Oh good, you're home,' she said.

'Just heading out to fencing,' I informed her.

'Oh buzznuckle, I'm dying to hear about your dress.'

'I didn't get one.'

'Seriously? It's only a week till your party.'

I groaned and pulled a face at her. 'Everything looks like a sack on me.' I stared enviously at her curves.

'Do you want me to go shopping with you tonight?'

'I'm working tonight.' Even though I knew I needed to find a dress, I was secretly relieved I had a reason not to go. I'd been demoralised enough for one day already. 'Better go, I'm running late for fencing.'

She pouted and then blew me a kiss. I lifted my wand and said, 'Bye. Clearius communius.' Her beautiful face disappeared, leaving me staring at my sweaty one. Even for July it was warm.

I wound the car windows down and turned the radio up, enjoying the warm summer breeze ruffling my hair.

I grabbed my bag and hurried in to change. Most of the others were already waiting when I emerged. I ran my eye along them looking for my friend Thomas, and that was when I saw her.

Isgranelda stood off to the side, a sour look on her face as she ran a finger over the point of her weapon. She pulled her finger away, squeezing the tip till a drop of blood welled.

What was she doing there? Was she *trying* to ruin my life?

'All right everybody.' Henry Lipton, our fencing teacher, moved to the middle of the room. 'Gather round.'

Thomas stood beside me as we gathered into a group around Henry. 'You got a dog?' he asked.

'I got a familiar.'

He stared at Scruffy for a few seconds. 'Cool.'

I could feel Isgranelda's gaze from the opposite side of the circle. Normally that would have made me nervous but suddenly I didn't care. I was sick of being bullied. I was sick of being scared. I met her eyes and gave her a small, tight smile. Her eyes narrowed in response as she examined me.

'Today we are going to practise all-combat fencing,' Henry said.

Some of the students around the circle let out a groan. All-combat fencing - where anything was allowed - could be violent. There were often injuries that required a trip to the Broken Bone Section of the hospital. Even though the medics there could heal you straight away, it didn't take away from the fact that the initial injury, and the healing, were painful.

'Who'd like to go first?' He looked around for a volunteer.

'I will.' I stepped forward and looked at Isgranelda, raising an eyebrow in a silent dare.

'Very good Isadora. Who wants to challenge her?' Henry asked.

'I will,' Isgranelda growled, wrenching her weapon from its guard. 'Okay?' she asked, holding it up for me to view.

She held an epee - a slim, flexible sword. I preferred the sabre, which could be used for cutting as well as thrusting, but I had issued the challenge and couldn't back out now.

'Sure,' I said, aiming for nonchalance. Thomas handed me his epee, picked up Scruffy, and joined the rest of the students backing away from us. It wasn't uncommon for an onlooker to suffer collateral damage when all-combat fencing became fierce.

'Izzy.' I could hear Thomas whispering from behind me. 'What are you doing?'

'Standing up for myself,' I hissed back.

Truth be told, I didn't know what had gotten into me. All I knew was that I wanted to beat her so badly I could taste it. I could hear my blood thrumming through my veins but I felt strangely calm.

'To the death?' she asked.

'Of course,' I said, shrugging.

Now before you freak out, let me explain. To the death didn't mean that one of us was going to die. It meant that we didn't want to score points for successful touches.

We wanted to fight until one of us had the other in a position that would have resulted in their death, if not for the impotent nature of our weapons. It meant we wanted to fight hard and we wanted to fight dirty. It wasn't something I normally looked forward to.

We moved over to the fighting mat amongst a haze of students' whispers. Isgranelda flexed her arms and rolled her shoulders. I gulped as I stared at her. I hadn't noticed how muscly she was before.

Henry rubbed his hands together and said, 'Excellent. Fight hard and fight clean.'

Yeah right.

Looking for the easy kill, Isgranelda launched herself through the air. I dodged to the side, felt her blade whiz past my head, and then, as her momentum carried her past me, I kicked her in the back. She turned and launched another attack. I backed steadily away from her as I parried her blows.

Left, left, right. Left, right, right. Left, right, left.

On her next right, I dived towards her, rolling beneath her blade and sweeping her legs out from under her as I went past. I bounced lightly to my feet and waited for her to gain hers. She was fuming.

'Don't fight mad,' Henry called out.

She ignored him, letting out an almighty roar as she attacked. I caught her blade on mine and deflected it; turning slightly at the last second to kick her in the stomach while she was still off balance. She growled and swept her weapon through a flurry of motion.

I moved in time with her, breathing steadily as I defended myself. It was as if she made every move a second after I realised she was going to. She was working faster and faster, swinging and slashing while I weaved and parried. I felt like we were dancing to a tune that only we could hear.

She made a desperate thrust at my neck and I slipped sideways and around to her back, bringing the tip of my weapon up towards her spine. Before I could claim the win, she whipped around, dodging to the side and bringing her blade low to strike my legs. Without thinking, I jumped into the air, flipping through a somersault to land back on my feet. A triumphant smile raced across her face - gone so fast I wondered if I had imagined it.

I had let her take the lead for too long. It was my turn to attack. I flowed towards her, my blade whistling through the air. She blocked each of my moves. We parried and struck, dodging and weaving till our limbs were a blur. The triumphant smile back on her face, she met me blow for blow. I could feel new strength flowing into my muscles, new skill imbedding into my mind. But I didn't stop to think about what was happening.

She thrust toward my throat and I cartwheeled backwards, kicking her hard in the stomach as I went. She should have been recovering from that kick. She should have been too winded to speak, let alone move, but the moment I was upright I could feel the tip of her epee pressed against the side of my neck.

I froze. How was that even possible? She had been in front of me and now she was behind. I heard her let out a low chuckle as she stroked the weapon down my throat. The rest of the class seemed as stunned as I was, silent as they stared at the two of us.

Finally Henry broke the silence, his eyes slightly wide as he clapped his hands together and said, 'Touché.'

I pushed away from her and turned around. The smile was gone but her eyes shone triumphantly.

'I don't know how you did that,' I said, 'but it won't work next time.'

'Ahhhh.' She leaned towards me and snapped her teeth together a few times. 'It bites.'

I backed away from her and into Thomas.

'Freaky much?' he murmured as she brushed past us. When she had gone he grasped my arm and said, 'That was amazing.'

'Me getting handed my arse was amazing?'

'No, but that somersault was. And since when can you do backflips?'

'I've always…' I stopped and stared at him.

I'd never done a backflip in my life. I had been too tall and gangly to be co-ordinated enough for gymnastics. Yet when I'd been fighting her it had all felt so natural.

***

The first thing I saw when I got to work was Mum seated in one of the booths with Sabby's Mum.

'Hi Aunty Grindella.' I leant over and kissed them before heading out the back. Throwing an apron over my head, I tied the strings behind me and then went back to the common area to begin taking drinks orders. The food wouldn't start for another half an hour.

Everything was progressing swimmingly till just before my break when Bob, one of the regulars, yelled out, 'Hey Izzy, heard you got your powers. How come you're still hand-delivering those drinks?'

All of the other witches, positioned at strategic locations, used their wands to transport their trays. Only Sally, a human, and I were hand-delivering ours.

'Umm, Bob, let's just say you'd probably prefer me to do it like this,' I said.

'Nonsense,' he roared. He had consumed quite a bit of Elves' Elixir and his cheeks were flushed. 'Who wants to see Izzy do her stuff?'

The rest of the crowd, who had been getting rowdier as the night went on, took up the cause. 'Izzy, Izzy,' they chanted, some of them banging their mugs on the table. The band had been playing a lively jig. Now, it screeched to a halt, everyone in the pub turning to watch me.

Mum was whispering to Grindella, probably telling her about the chair episode from the night before. I saw them hold hands across the table and then she looked up and winked at me.

Oh thank the Great Dark Sky. They were going to use their powers to control mine.

Turning confidently to the crowd, I held up my hand. 'All right, all right,' I said, placing my tray on the table nearest to me. It held eight large mugs of ale and two glasses of Faery Water. Pulling my wand out of my hair I concentrated on the tray.

'Risius trayius,' I said.

The tray leapt off the table and smashed into the ceiling, splintering the glasses and mugs. I shrieked and threw my hands up as liquid and glass flew towards me. The air above solidified, like a sheet of glass, and the falling debris bounced harmlessly onto its surface.

The entire pub was silent, staring at the pool of ale floating above me on the invisible shield.

Finally Bob broke the silence, 'Well ain't that something,' he said. 'If you don't mind though Izzy, I'd prefer you to hand-deliver my drinks.'

The band struck up again, everybody turned back to their conversations, and just like that, it was over.

I kept my hands in the air till Mum came to rescue me.

'I thought you had it covered,' I whispered.

'So did we,' she muttered as she banished the mess to a bin in the corner of the room.

'What happened?' I lowered my hands, watching as the shield disappeared.

'Our spell had no effect on yours. We didn't even feel your magic.'

'How can that be?' All spells have a weave and a flow about them that another witch can detect. It's what makes spell duelling possible. If you are fast enough you can feel a spell and counteract it.

'I don't know. But the sooner we find out about it the better.'

'Yeah, I'm getting sick of throwing things at the ceiling.'

'Why do you keep trying to levitate things?'

'I'm too scared to try anything else.'

'Don't. Not until we get professional help.'

Professional help?

Deciding it was a good time to take my break, I slid into the booth beside Mum. Grindella leaned over the table towards me and asked, 'So Izzy, are you looking forward to next Saturday?'

'Sort of,' I said, squirming at the thought. It was customary for the whole village to turn out for a witch or warlock's eighteenth birthday. Mum had organised a marquee for the field behind the house.

Sabby's party had been the month before. She had looked amazing in a red, velvet dress that'd clung to her like Gladwrap on a glass. At the rate I was going I was going to be wearing jeans and a tank top.

All too quickly my break was over and I was back to work. The others left not long after that. Scruffy curled up in a corner near the kitchen and fell asleep. When my shift was finally over I stood and watched him for a while before waking him. He looked so cute.

I had been relieved at the lack of fuss the pub's patrons had made over the fact that my familiar was a dog. I had expected shock but instead had been met with curiosity. It let me hope that things would work out after all.

The floating chariot was hovering outside the house when I got home. As I tiptoed underneath it I could hear Grams giggling. I put my hands over my ears and bumped the front door with my knee, urging Eric to let me in before they heard me.

'Izzy, is that you?' Grandma Bella called from above.

'Yes Grams,' I said, turning to face them whilst trying not to see anything. 'How was your night?'

'Just wonderful,' Grams sighed. 'The whole evening has been wonderful.'

'It's not over yet,' Lionel rumbled.

Grams laughed wickedly in response.

The door popped open behind me and I rushed inside before I heard anything that would render me unable to sleep.

I placed Scruffy's new bed on the floor. Once I was sure he was comfortable, I climbed wearily into mine. My head had just touched the pillow when I felt him jump up beside me. He turned around a few times, scraping the covers up underneath himself, and then snuggled into my back. I had one last sleepy thought that I should move him back onto his own bed, and then my mind slipped away from my body and into a deep, dark sleep.

Chapter Four

Who's Your Daddy?

The front doorbell woke me early the next morning. Either someone had their finger jammed on it, or it was stuck. I was hoping it was the latter. A finger jammed on a doorbell never boded good news.

Scruffy jumped from the bed and ran down the stairs, barking as he went. I peered blurrily at the bedside clock. It was just past seven. Who would be ringing our bell at this time?

'Hang on,' I could hear Mum yell from her quarters.

I yawned as I pictured her pulling on her fluffy, pink bathrobe and running her hands through her hair to make herself presentable, and then I fell asleep again.

'Izzy.' Mum was standing in the door to my bedroom. 'There's someone here to see you.'

'What?' I mean *really*, I was on holidays. No-one should have to get out of bed this early on holidays.

'Didn't you hear the doorbell?'

'Who is it?'

'If I told you, you wouldn't believe it,' she said, shaking her head.

I pulled a robe over my nightie and headed down the stairs after her. I could hear her muttering, 'And me in my nightgown and bathrobe.'

There was a tall, regal woman outside the open front door. She tapped her foot as she looked around with an unimpressed look on her face. Mum and I moved onto the front porch to stand opposite her.

'Please your Majesty, won't you come in and have a cup of tea?' Mum asked.

Your Majesty?

The lady bent a little at the waist and peered into the depths of our house before sniffing. 'I really don't think so.' Her face darkened as she turned her attention to me. 'So young lady, what have you got to say for yourself?'

'Ummm, hi,' I said.

Both her eyebrows went up and the look in her eyes hardened. She turned and spoke over her shoulder, 'You didn't tell me she was a smart-arse.'

Trying not to take offence at the smart-arse comment I peered past her. No-one was there.

Mum looked as confused as I was as she swept a hand in my direction and said, 'Your Majesty, may I present to you my daughter Isadora.'

I wasn't sure what the correct etiquette for meeting royalty was. In a panic, I made a clumsy half-bow, half-curtsy, while hoping my robe didn't reveal too much excess skin.

'Isadora,' continued Mum, 'may I present Her Majesty, Queen Eloise of the Faeries.'

Queen of the Faeries?

Queen Eloise studied my stunned expression. 'You didn't know who I was?'

'I had a bit of an idea,' I mumbled, not wanting to look totally stupid. I waved a hand in the general direction of my head. 'Your ears gave it away.'

'Hummphh.' Queen Eloise didn't seem very happy with my answer. She looked at Mum and said, 'Your daughter has been courting my son without our Royal consent.'

'What?' Mum and I both exclaimed at the same time.

'That's ludicrous,' I added.

'Yes, well,' the Queen continued, 'it seems you have been doing it without your knowledge, but it will stop from this moment on.'

I noticed Scruffy sniffing around the bottom of her robes.

'Isadora?' Mum looked at me.

'I have no idea what she's talking about.' It really wasn't going to go down well if he peed on her.

Queen Eloise let out a snort of derision. Scruffy looked up and grasped the soft material of her skirts with his teeth, letting out a grumbly growl whilst pulling on them. She tugged at her clothing trying to dislodge him.

'I don't.' I tried not to laugh at the bizarre spectacle unfolding between the Queen and Scruffy; she tug-o-warred with him for possession of her clothing whilst he tried to drag her away from me.

I rushed forwards and picked him up, placing him at my feet. 'Stay,' I whispered. He let out one more little ruffing growl before settling down to investigate the intricacy of his testicles.

'I don't see how what you are suggesting is even possible,' Mum said.

'Dream-walkers are rare these days. My son is one and it would appear that your daughter is as well.'

'So you're saying I'm dating him while I'm asleep?' The thought was preposterous.

She nodded her head.

'If what you say is true, and I have been dating your son without my own knowledge, then how am I meant to stop it?'

'I know you're listening,' she said after a heartbeat's pause, 'come here this instant.'

Just as I was starting to think that maybe the Queen was a bit wacko, a head appeared, floating in mid-air.

'Whizbang,' I yelped in fright. I could hear the Queen tisking at my use of bad language.

The face gave me a devastating smile and said, 'Hello Izzy.'

'Izzy?' Mum asked me.

For one prickly second I knew him. But then it was gone and I was looking at a stranger.

'All the way please Aethan,' commanded the Queen.

The face sighed, then a hand appeared beside it and moved as if pushing an invisible curtain aside. His other hand pushed in the opposite direction and all of a sudden the head had a body. I could feel myself blush as my eyes roamed over him. Leather pants encased his legs, and a fur vest, cinched at the waist with more leather, covered his chest. Well, it *sort* of covered his chest.

I gulped as I stared at his pectoral and abdominal muscles. This was no mere boy – this was a man; a hard, muscular man. *Way* too much man for me.

I licked my suddenly-dry lips as I met his eyes. 'Hi,' I said.

'So you *do* remember,' Queen Eloise said.

I shook my head. 'Maybe it will help if you tell me where we met.'

'In a field by a river.' The look in his eyes was so intense that I blushed and looked away.

'Surely,' Mum said to Queen Eloise, 'you cannot hold Isadora responsible for something that is happening while she is asleep.'

'I hold her totally responsible. She is grasping beyond her means, seducing my son so that he will have to marry her. As if an heir to the Faery Throne would marry a *witch!*'

'Whoa,' I said, putting my hand in the air, 'who said *anything* about *marriage?*'

'I can assure you,' Mum's voice was angry, 'that Isadora is not that kind of girl. She's never even had a boyfriend before.'

I groaned and closed my eyes. Mum was making me sound like a right loser. I didn't want to look like a loser in front of this man.

'Mother,' Aethan said, 'how many times do I have to tell you that it's not like that?'

'Well, what is it like.'

'It's…' He stopped talking and gasped as a spasm roiled over his body. His back arched and his hands clenched into fists as he bit his bottom lip. It was over within a few seconds, but his face was covered in a fine sheen of sweat. He took a deep breath, rolled his eyes to the sky and straightened his shoulders. 'Okay, it is like that,' he said.

What in the Dark Sky had just happened? Was he epileptic?

Queen Eloise's cheeks coloured. 'I've always been softer on you than your elder siblings. But your behaviour has become intolerable. Spurning suitable suitors for ***this***.' She spat out the last word and flung an angry arm in my direction.

I threw mine up in defence and the air in front of me hardened till it resembled a piece of Perspex. I was so shocked I let my arms fall back to my side. The air shimmered and returned to normal.

Queen Eloise's eyes widened. 'What did you just do?'

'Nothing.' It was just like in the Lodge the night before. But *this* time I didn't have a wand in my hand.

She moved gracefully toward me. 'May I?' she asked, holding a hand up towards my head.

I wasn't sure what she was about to do but I doubted she meant to harm me. I nodded my assent. She brushed back my hair and looked at my ears, then stared intently into my eyes. She picked up my arm and examined my fingers and nails, then placed her hands on either side of my head and, closing her eyes, appeared to go into some kind of trance. Just when I was getting really freaked out, she opened her eyes.

'Someone has not been entirely truthful,' she said in an ominous voice.

'I don't remember anything.' I backed away from her.

'I'm not talking to you. I'm talking to your mother.' She stepped away from me towards Mum. 'I knew for her to be a dream-walker there must be faery blood in her, but this I did not expect. Tell me, how is it that Royal blood runs in her veins?'

Mum's face took on a look of horror. She stared at Queen Eloise, two spots of colour spreading over her cheeks, and then she dropped her eyes to the ground. 'He said he loved me.'

'Mother? Who are you talking about?'

'Your father.'

'My father was Sidney Mesmerer, a warlock you met at a Full Moon Party. You were to be married but he died in an unfortunate cauldron accident.' I parroted the words she had told me many, many times. Even as they left my mouth I heard how silly they sounded. 'Ahhhhh,' I said, in sudden understanding.

'May I request the name of Isadora's real father?' Queen Eloise seemed unmoved by Mum's remorse. I decided I didn't like her very much.

Mum pushed back her shoulders and looked up. 'Alexus Gabrielle,' she said.

'Great Uncle Alex?' Aethan asked, amusement playing around the edges of his mouth.

'He always has been a bit of a ladies' man,' Queen Eloise said with a nod of her head. Then turning to me she said, 'Well, cousin.'

'Cousin?'

'It would appear so. I still blame you for this mess. You need to gain control of your powers. And I mean *all* your powers. You cannot go dream-walking with a blatant lack of knowledge of what you are doing.'

She turned her gaze to Mum. 'Prunella, I apologise on behalf of my Uncle, his behaviour towards you was callous. This, however, changes things. Any female of Royal blood may court an heir to the throne. Even though I don't like it,' she stopped and sniffed loudly, 'I must give my permission for your daughter to court my son.'

I tried to hide my panic. It was fine to ogle a man like Aethan from afar, but I was sure my mouth would disconnect from my brain if I tried to have a conversation with him. Let alone *court* him. That word put a *whole* new level of pressure on the situation.

'We will leave you to your daily preparations.' She looked up and down at our bathrobes. 'Come Aethan.' She made the same sideways movement with her hands we had seen him do, took a step forward, and disappeared. Her voice echoed back to us, 'We will be in touch.'

'Umm, goodbye,' I said to Aethan.

I felt my heartbeat accelerate as his stare pierced me. He took a few steps forward till we were close enough to touch. 'Remember,' he commanded, touching me on the end of my nose with a finger. 'It will make things *much* easier.' Then he turned and disappeared.

'Holy moley,' I said when I had regained control of my voice box.

'So,' Mum said, 'what would you like for breakfast?'

'What do I want for breakfast?' I turned to stare at her.

'Aren't you hungry?'

'Well yes. But what I would like for breakfast is a big plate of the truth, served up with a side dish of apology.'

'So you're not going to just forget about this?' The look I gave her must have spoken volumes because she said, 'I guess not. Well come on, you may as well have a shower while I make some pancakes, and then I'll tell you the whole sordid story.'

She was obviously sucking up to me. Pancakes were my absolute favourite.

'Good enough for me,' I said, looking around for Scruffy. 'Mum's cooking pancakes,' I informed him as he snuffled around a bush. He let out an enthusiastic bark and followed me inside and up the stairs to my room where I stripped off my nightie and jumped in the shower.

I was pissed at Mum and not quite sure what to make of the whole situation. But two days ago I had feared I was to be left powerless, a total reject in the witch society, and today I found myself with both witch and faery powers, and a cousin to the Fae Queen. When I compared the two situations I found that, for once, I was on the side with the greener grass.

***

Grandma Bella had emerged from her rooms when I finally arrived in the kitchen. She was sipping a coffee with a dreamy look on her face and pink feathered slippers on her feet. Cyril was lying on the table, coiled up in a patch of sun.

'Pancakes?' she asked, nodding her head at Mum spooning batter into the frying pan. 'What's the special occasion?'

'It's not every day that a girl finds out she's half-Fae.'

Grandma Bella's face went pale.

'I guess it explains my dark hair though,' I said. Most witches had red hair, and if it wasn't exactly red, it was a variant of it.

Grams started coughing on her sip of tea.

'And how tall I am.' I leant over and whacked her on the back a couple of times.

'We're talking about *you?'* she said when she could breathe again.

I watched Mum flip a couple of pancakes onto a plate. I could feel saliva pooling. 'Who did you think I was talking about?'

'Oh nobody dear, I'm a bit fuzzy this morning. Drank a bit too much Fizzy Lizard last night.'

'Ughhhh. That's disgusting.'

'It's not *really* made from lizards.'

Mum approached the table with a platter piled high with pancakes. I jumped up and grabbed the cutlery and the maple syrup.

'Where's Scruffy's?' I asked, counting the pancakes. He was sitting patiently in the kitchen watching Mum with his big, brown eyes.

'He had his while you were in the shower.'

'But he was lying in the bathroom while I was in the shower,' I said.

'No, he was down here scoffing pancakes.'

I looked at Scruffy with narrowed eyes and then shrugged my shoulders. I had more important questions to ask this morning than why my familiar seemed to be in two places at once. But I wasn't quite sure which question to ask first so I started with the obvious one. Why don't you tell me about my father?'

'Yes,' Grams leant forward, her blue eyes bright with merriment. 'Someone was a naughty girl.'

'Where do you want me to start?' Mum asked, ignoring Grams.

'Well,' I stopped and swallowed my mouthful of pancake, 'how did you meet him?'

'I met him at the annual Tri-Race Convention. He was standing in as head of the faeries, and I was there as a reporter. I managed to get a one-on-one interview with him.'

Grandma let out a snort. 'One-on-one all right.'

'Mother,' Mum said, 'it wasn't like that.'

'What was is like?' I asked.

She paused for a minute, a far-off look in her eyes. 'Well, in retrospect, it probably was like that,' she conceded. 'He was so... raw.'

I looked at her with my eyebrows raised. 'Raw?'

'Faery warriors,' Grams reached out for another pancake, 'they're the embodiment of everything male. There's a wildness to them. It's hard to explain unless you've met one of them.'

I gulped as I thought of Aethan. Raw, wild, manly. That about summed it up.

'Anyway,' Mum continued, 'he swept me off my feet. I fell in love with him, but when the convention was over I never saw him again.'

'Oh Mum,' I said. Even after all those years there was still pain in her voice.

She smiled and said, 'I got *you,* so it was all worth it.'

'Faeries make incredible lovers,' Grams said, reaching for another pancake, 'or so I've heard.'

'So why,' I asked, trying not to think too much about *that*, 'did you make up Sidney Mesmerer?'

'Alexus was Santanas Gabrielle's brother.'

I froze in the act of picking up a pancake. '*The* Santanas Gabrielle?' I was guessing there was only one.

Mum nodded her head.

Breathless, I sat back in my chair. The War Faery was my Uncle? The faery who'd tortured and killed thousands of people was my Uncle? I was suddenly *very* glad his soul was entombed in stone.

Grams shot Mum a wild look. 'Alexus Gabrielle is Isadora's *father?*'

Mum nodded. 'Did you meet him when you worked in Isilvitania?'

'Once or twice.'

'You used to work in Isilvitania?' *That* was something I hadn't known.

Grams nodded her head. 'A long, long time ago. Before your mother was born.'

'Does… Alexus know about me?' I couldn't make myself use the word father on a total stranger.

'I never told him.'

I put my fork down. Suddenly, pancakes didn't taste so good. 'What do you think courting Aethan is going to entail?'

'I'm sorry,' Grams said, 'did I miss something?'

'Not much,' I waved a hand in the air. 'Apparently I've been hanging out with Aethan Gabrielle in my dreams.' I raised my cup to take a sip of my tea.

Hanging out? I imagined some of the things we might have been doing together and the warmth of a blush erupted on my cheeks.

'*The* Aethan Gabrielle? Second-in-line to the throne and Champion of the Faeries?'

My tea lodged in the back of my throat. I coughed and spluttered till I could breathe again. Second-in-line to the throne? Champion of the Faeries? Great Dark Sky, what had I dream-walked myself into?

'Wonder what Queen Eloise will have to say about that?' Grams had an amused look on her face.

'Thanks to my faery blood she had to give us permission to court,' I said.

'She was *here*?' Grams stared at the front door, a wild light in her eyes.

'You missed her,' Mum said, hopping up to get more pancakes.

'Dear me,' Grams said, smoothing down the already smooth tablecloth, 'you *have* been busy.' She shot another look at the front door. 'I was wondering who you were holding out for.'

'Grams!'

'Don't even think about it,' Grams replied, which made absolutely no sense until I realised that her familiar had uncoiled himself and was peering over the edge of the table at Scruffy.

'We're going to have to let them sort it out or it will be a constant problem,' Mum said.

Cyril slithered further over the edge, flicking his tongue as he tasted the air around his victim. Scruffy stared at Cyril with a wide, doggy grin as he released his own secret weapon. A smell, so potent my eyes watered, rolled over us.

Poor Cyril, his tongue still out of his mouth, went limp. The weight of his head dragged the length of his body slithering over the edge of the table to the floor, where he lay in a pile of tumbled coils.

When the air had cleared enough, we continued the conversation. 'So Mum, the courting thing, what does it all mean?'

'It's like dating, but a bit more formal.'

'What if I don't want to date him?'

'Don't want to date *that*?' Mum asked.

'What woman of flesh and blood would not want to date *that?*' Grams fanned herself with her hands. 'I saw him at the Tri-Race Convention a few years ago. Hubba hubba.' A knock at the front door disturbed her and she leapt out of her seat like a scared rabbit and bustled off towards her rooms.

I shook my head at her eccentricity as I hopped up to let Sabby in. She was taking me shopping for a dress.

'Pancakes?' she said, peering past me to the diningroom table.

'Help yourself.'

'I shouldn't, not if we're going clothes shopping. I might bloat.'

I burst out laughing and pushed her towards the table. 'You don't know the meaning of the word bloat.'

Scruffy waddled over to her, a pathetic look on his face as he eyed off her plate.

'Now *he*,' I said, 'knows all about bloating.'

We didn't leave for the shops until I had filled Sabby in on the morning's developments and then answered about a zillion questions. Even after we got to the Eynsford Department Store she kept plying me with new ones. Most of them were about Aethan, and most of them I couldn't answer, but all of a sudden she said, 'When are you trying out for the Advanced Academy of Witches?'

'I'm not.' I held a dress up in front of me while I studied myself in the mirror. 'What were they thinking when they designed this?' It had bows on the hips *and* shoulders.

'What do you mean you're not?' She shoved another dress at me. It was as bad as the previous one.

'Which word didn't you understand?'

'Very funny. Why aren't you going to try out?'

'I wouldn't get in.'

'You don't know that.'

'I can't control my powers. And besides, nothing there interests me.' The problem with *that* was that I didn't know *what* interested me.

I wasn't sure if her scandalised look was for the dress I had pulled off the rack or what I'd just said. I was guessing it was for what I'd said.

'Come on,' I said before she could launch into a spiel on how wonderful the college was, 'there's nothing here that suits me.' I dragged her from the shop and she thankfully left the subject alone.

'Coffee?' she asked instead.

A man, dressed like Aethan had been – all fur and leather, caught my eye. He sat at a table in the middle of the shopping centre and cleaned his nails with a dagger. A long scar ran down the side of his face and a pile of brochures sat on the table in front of him. He didn't look very interested in handing them out.

'Hang on,' I said to Sabby.

I approached him warily and stared at the brochures. He lowered his dagger and eyed me through his thick, bushy eyebrows.

'Nothing for you here,' he said.

'How do you know that?'

He had a menacing feel about him. Even though he was sitting still, I had no doubt he could snap me like a twig.

'You're a girl,' he said, starting to clean his nails again.

I reached out and picked up a brochure. 'Border Guards?'

'That's right,' he said, not even looking up.

'What do you do?'

'We guard the borders between our magical world and the others.'

'I might be interested in being a Border Guard.' I might be, if Aethan were one.

'You need faery blood.'

'Well, I guess this is my lucky day. My dad is all faery.'

He pointed to the scar on his face with the tip of his dagger. 'I got this from a troll.'

I pointed at a scar on my leg. 'I got this falling off a bicycle.'

He let out a snort and I realised I had been dismissed.

I stuffed the brochure into my jeans pocket and made my way back to where Sabina was staring at handbags.

'Who was that?' she asked.

'Hmmm?'

'That man?'

'Oh, a Border Guard.' I held my breath, praying to the Great Dark Sky that she would leave the subject alone.

She stared at me for a second, her eyebrows lowered, and then said, 'Come and see this handbag. It would look great with that navy-blue dress you tried on.'

'You mean the skin-tight one?' I let out an inaudible sigh of relief.

I had already fielded too many questions about Aethan that morning. I was never going to hear the end of it if I admitted I'd taken a brochure because the gruff man had been dressed like him. That was way past sad and all the way to the Land of Pathetic.

Chapter Five

Some Days Aren't Worth Getting Out Of Bed For

'I can't wear this,' I said to Sabina. The navy-blue dress was so tight I was finding it hard to breathe.

'Nonsense, you look gorgeous.'

'But it's so…'

'Grown-up?' Sabby had a stubborn look on her face.

The dress was very grown-up. That was the problem. I wasn't used to wearing clothing that showed the exact contour of my body.

'It's not the dress. It's me.' That part was true.

'Well perhaps you should have found the time to buy *yourself* a dress.' Sabina's voice had taken on a dangerous tone. A tone I knew all too well.

If I were being totally honest with myself, I would have had to admit that I looked fantastic. Sabby had spent hours on my hair and make-up, and the dark-haired beauty that stared back at me was someone I had not met before. I wasn't sure if I could do her justice.

And the dress? Well, the dress was something else entirely. Navy-blue silk hugged me to my knees. The bodice would have been strapless if not for the two spaghetti-thin straps that graced my shoulders. The crystal necklace and earrings Grams and Mum had given me for my birthday were going to complement it perfectly.

'I can't walk in these shoes.' I mean as if I weren't tall enough *without* the sky-high, silver stilettos.

'Get used to them,' Sabby barked.

'I'm sorry,' I said. 'It's not that I don't appreciate everything you've done for me.' The look on her face softened. 'And the dress is perfect, and my hair looks amazing. You could get a job as a stylist.'

The scowl slid off her face and was replaced by a small smile. I sighed inwardly with relief. The last thing I needed at my party was a sulky Sabina; I was relying on her to act as a pseudo-hostess.

Scruffy sat near the door to my bedroom, his mouth open in a doggy grin. 'You wouldn't know I washed him this morning,' I said to Sabina.

'You wouldn't know you'd ever washed him.'

And then I saw it. His old, black, studded collar sat snugly around his neck. 'Agghhh,' I said, as I tottered towards him on my dangerously high heels.

'What's wrong?'

'That's the third time I've put his new collar on.'

'I thought his new collar was red.'

'It is,' I said, as I ferretted around in the bathroom bin. I emerged with his shiny, red collar in my hand. '*This* is his new collar.'

'So who keeps putting his old collar on?'

'No-one.'

Initially I had thought Mum or Grams must have been doing it, but they had both professed innocence, and I knew that no-one but Sabby and I had been in my bathroom all morning.

'That's one weird familiar,' Sabby said.

'Yoohoo,' Grams called from downstairs.

'Come on up,' I yelled back.

'What do you think?' Grams asked from the top of the staircase.

I watched in astonishment as she settled a feathered mask over her eyes.

'Really?' I asked.

'You don't like it?' The black and white striped feathers matched her current hair-do and black velvet dress. I noticed that Cyril was also black and white striped.

'No, no, it's just an interesting choice.' I had already offended Sabby this morning; I didn't want to add Grams to that list.

'I could wear this one.' She held up a sequined gold one.

'The black and white one is better,' Sabby said. She didn't seem to be at all disturbed by Gram's decision to wear a mask to my birthday party.

'Yippee, the guests are starting to arrive,' Grams said as she peered out my window. She hurried back down the stairs and I heard the front door close a few moments later.

Eeeek. The moment of truth. I managed to make it to the window without tripping over my own feet. I could see people in the distance winding their way down a narrow path to the large field behind our house. A huge marquee fluttered in the distance, its bright colours adding a festive feel to the otherwise green field. A banner, so large I could read it from where I was – Happy Birthday Isadora – hung over the opening. I knew there were also chairs and tables and a dance floor set up, but I didn't know *how* I was going to dance in these shoes.

'So,' Sabby said, 'is Aethan coming to the party?'

Great Dark Sky, the last thing I needed right at that moment was to think about Aethan. I was nervous enough about my party without throwing that into the mix.

I hadn't heard anything since that weird morning a week ago. Nothing about the courting and nothing about my training. I wasn't sure which I was more disappointed about.

'I don't know,' I said, turning away from the window. 'Mum said she sent an invitation to the faeries.'

'They didn't R.S.V.P? How rude.'

I heard a shout from the field. It was quickly followed by a scream that had the hairs on the back of my neck doing an impression of a group of prairie dogs. I spun back toward the window, falling awkwardly as one of my shoes got twisted in the rug. I hardly felt the pain in my ankle as I stared out over the field.

People were no longer meandering down the path towards my party. Now they ran across the field, away from the field, up the path; they ran anywhere that they could.

Goblins chased them, their cruel swords hacking and slashing at anyone not quick enough to get away. I could see a couple of bodies lying in front of the marquee.

Goblins? Here in sleepy Eynsford?

'Grams,' I said. 'Oh Great Dark Sky, not Grams.'

I yanked the shoes off and ran, as fast as my dress would allow, to the front door. Mum came running towards me from her rooms.

I picked up Scruffy and placed him in Mum's arms. 'Stay here,' I said to her and Sabby. 'Eric will keep you all safe. Don't let Scruffy out.' A battle with goblins was no place for my little, white familiar.

There was a moment's resistance as I twisted the front door knob. 'Please,' my voice caught on the word. 'Please, you have to let me get Grams.'

The resistance lasted for a moment more and then the knob twisted in my hand. 'Thank you,' I whispered as I raced through the doorway. I heard Scruffy barking behind me.

Which way had Grams gone? The straight path down to the field that was steep and slippery, or the long way that twisted through the edge of the trees?

I had to hope she wouldn't have wanted to risk a chance of slipping in her gown, and gone the long way round. At least then she would have a chance to run and hide in the trees. I headed for the start of the path.

Lily Templeton burst from the trees in front of me, a goblin not three paces behind. Her eyes were wild, her mouth wide open, but no screams came from her. She was conserving her energy for the only two things she could: running and praying.

I looked around for a weapon, grabbing a thick branch off the ground before ducking behind a tree. As she ran past me, I stepped out and swung the branch at the goblin's head. It made a satisfying clonk as it connected with his skull. He went down with a roar and I jumped on top of him and thwacked him again and again until finally, he stopped twitching. Panting, I leant on my branch, trying not to puke as I stared at his blood-spattered body.

I had seen pictures of goblins of course; had even seen one on the news once. And I'd heard countless stories about them at the Toasted Toadstool. But *nothing* had prepared me for *this.*

He was huge; at least a foot and a half taller than my six foot. His skin was a dark-coffee colour, his long hair matted into dreadlocks that cascaded down to his waist. He wore a leather loincloth with a strap that ran across his chest and over one shoulder. The leather strap was decorated with small bones. An ugly, curved dagger was sheathed at his waist, another dangled from his lifeless fingers. But the scariest things were his teeth; filed to points, they looked capable of tearing flesh from limbs.

With a start I realised I had been staring at the goblin for longer than was safe. Lily Templeton had disappeared, probably unaware that the creature was no longer chasing her, and I had to find Grams.

I plucked the dagger from his hand and hacked at my dress, ripping the side-seam up high enough that I could run unencumbered. Then, with the dagger in one hand and the branch in the other, I advanced slowly towards the path. I kept to the edge of the tree line and watched for goblins.

It didn't take me long to find them.

Two appeared in the trees in front of me, walking slowly through the long grass as they searched. I saw a flash of black and white feathers off to the left and realised Grams was there, crouching behind a shrub. I bit my lip in frustration. The goblins were between her and me, heading off to her left. Was it possible they wouldn't see her? I was suddenly absurdly glad she hadn't decided to go with the gold-sequinned mask.

I could hear screams from the village and smell smoke in the air, but I stayed still as I watched them. One suddenly froze and, raising his head, sniffed the air. He put a hand on the other goblin's arm and said something in a low, guttural tone.

I looked anxiously towards where Grams was hiding. The black and white feathers had disappeared from view, but it was towards her that the sniffing goblin turned. He put his hand on a dagger handle and pulled it clear; the blade rasping out of the sheath on his chest. The second goblin laughed softly as he pulled his own dagger free.

Oh Dark Sky. They could smell Grams. I might be able to take on one, but two? I may as well stab myself now and be done with it. But she was my Grandmother, and I wasn't going to stand still and watch her die.

My heart beat wildly as I crept up behind them. One step closer, another step. I had to move faster or they would make it to Grams before I got to them.

In the end it was my haste that undid me. Too busy watching them to look where I was stepping, my foot landed on a pointed stone. The sharp edge dug into my bare foot and I let out a small, 'Ow,' before I had realised it.

One of the goblins spun towards me, roaring as he advanced.

'Now, now,' I said as I backed hurriedly away, 'I wasn't really going to hurt you.' That was probably correct, but it wouldn't have been through a lack of trying.

The other goblin watched warily, eyeing the dagger in my hand. But I didn't have time to watch him, because the first one was already upon me. He plunged his dagger towards me. I let out a shriek and dived to the side as the blade whistled past my head.

I spun as I went, bringing the branch around like a baseball bat. It thumped into his mid-section and he bent at the waist. I clocked him over the head with it and kicked him to the side. He let out a growl and ran at me, crouched over like a footballer going in for a tackle.

I jumped into the air, spinning in a forward somersault over the top of him. He crashed headfirst into a tree, shaking his head like a big bull as he turned back towards me.

This one wasn't as easy to dispose of as the first one. It looked like I was going to have to use the blade. For some stupid reason I didn't mind the idea of clubbing him to death as much as I did the thought of knifing him. What part of his body should I aim for? His heart? But that was protected by his ribs. I would have to get in close which meant I would only get one go at it. I had to make it a killing strike.

I eyed the big beast as I circled around him, trying to work out the easiest way to kill him without allowing him to plunge his ugly weapon into me.

And then it came to me. His neck. I should aim for the side of his neck. There were arteries there. If I were lucky, I would get one.

I waited for him to charge me again. This time, instead of leaping into the air, I pirouetted to the side, my knife arm held out wide. The tip of the dagger ripped into the unexposed side of his neck and blood burst from him. I felt the warmth of it spray across me, tasted the saltiness on my tongue.

And then I felt the dagger of the second goblin pressed against my neck.

Stupid, stupid. I had totally forgotten about him. It was going to be the last mistake I ever made.

'Hey big boy,' Grams shouted.

I made use of her distraction to elbow him in the ribs and rip myself from his grasp. He snarled as he looked between me and Grams.

The first goblin lay on his side, blood spurting rhythmically from his wound. A pleased thought – that I had got an artery after all – flashed into my head; followed even swifter by the notion that it was ridiculous to have time to be pleased about such things.

'Over here,' I yelled as he started towards Grams.

I saw Grams lift her wand and flick it at him and he suddenly let out a snigger. The snigger turned to a giggle and then a full-on ugly laugh. He threw his head back and clutched his arms around his chest as if to contain his mirth.

I rushed to Gram's side. 'What did you do?'

'Hit him with a funny spell.'

The goblin collapsed to his knees, roaring with laughter as he pointed at his dead companion.

'Wouldn't have been my first choice.'

'It worked didn't it? You going to kill him?'

'I don't know if I can when he's so… helpless,' I said. 'Come on, I've got to get you back to the house.'

'Nonsense.' She started to walk towards the main part of the village. 'There are more goblins to deal with.'

Once Grams had her mind made up there was nothing I could do to change it. I grabbed another dagger from the dead goblin and chased after her.

'Here,' I said, handing it to her.

She shook her head and held her wand up. 'Why didn't you spell them?'

'Last night I tried to elevate a watermelon and it exploded.'

She paused at the side of Mr and Mrs Trill's house, peering around the edge of the building and up the street. 'Not such a bad fate for a goblin.'

She was right, but the problem was that even my mistakes were unpredictable. I could try the same spell three times with three totally different results. It was possible I could try a spell to freeze them and end up weaving flowers through their hair. I was going to have to rely on weapons to get through this.

'Come on.' She scuttled away from the house, across the street and paused behind a large oak near the post office. A couple of goblins were in the process of setting fire to the building.

Grams pointed her wand at them and a large jet of water burst from its tip. She let out a gleeful cackle as it smacked into them, putting out their fire. The one closest to us held his arms up, trying to shield his face from the flow. I raced towards him, bending low as I passed to cut the back of his ankles. I saw a wolf do that to a lamb once, and this was just as effective.

He bellowed in pain as he crashed to the ground, but his friend leapt over him, narrowly missing my throat with his dagger. I took off as fast as I could, quickly realising my attempt to outrun this goblin was doomed to fail. I could hear his grunting breath getting closer and closer.

I could spin and face him, but his momentum would very likely carry him through me. I would be lucky if he didn't gut me.

And then I saw the other goblins farther up the street. Swearing, I changed course, heading for the clock tower. I heard yelling behind me and realised I now had all of the goblins on my tail. This was turning out to be one hell of a birthday.

Glad I had taken up running as a hobby, but wishing I had concentrated on the sprinting part of the vocation, I broke into the square around the clock tower. A handful of men were already there, swords-in-hand as they battled a group of goblins.

'Incoming,' I yelled as I raced towards them.

I increased my speed, heading straight for the side of the clock tower. As I reached it, I lengthened my stride and ran up the side, pushing off and executing a backward somersault over the goblins. I landed behind them and hamstringed the two closest; swirling straight away to shove the dagger into a third one's neck. I felt the blade dig deeper than I had intended, catching as it struck bone. I leapt clear of his outstretched arms with only the branch to defend myself.

'Here,' one of the men yelled as he threw a sword hilt-first to me.

I grabbed it out of the air as the closest standing goblin turned towards me. I was used to lighter fencing swords, not this heavy, ungainly weapon. I hefted it with both hands and, using the same technique I had with the branch, I swung the blade towards the goblin. It struck home, into and then through his neck. Blood sprayed out in an arc as he fell to the ground. His severed head bounced a couple of times as it hit the pavement. The open eyes blinked once as they stared up at me.

'Gross,' I said, trying not to slip in the blood as I stepped around it.

The next goblin approached me more warily. He feigned a couple of times with his dagger and I slapped him away with my sword.

To be honest, I didn't know what the hell I was doing. I had no idea how to use this blade effectively and I was staring at it, wishing desperately it were a sabre, when all of a sudden it was. The shock almost ended my life as the goblin chose that exact moment to charge.

'Whizbang,' I yelped, diving to the ground. I brought the sabre up as a reflex and the tip of it pierced his side. He let out an 'Oooph,' and then fell to his knees, staring in confusion at his chest where the tip of my sabre had emerged.

'Nice,' one of the men said, kicking the goblin off my blade. 'But then you always did have style.' He was huge, with red, shaggy hair growing out of every part of his body. Even the area of his chest that his fur vest didn't cover was a carpet of red. 'Duck,' he said, and I realised in time that he wasn't talking about the winged variety.

I dropped to my knees and he swung his sword over the top of me. Warm liquid sprayed over the back of my neck and arms.

I looked over my shoulder. A goblin lay in a pool of blood. 'Thanks,' I said.

Black and white feathers caught my attention. Standing off to the side, Grams flicked her wand at a goblin. He immediately dropped his dagger, placed his arms in the air, and started to waltz to music only he could hear.

My shaggy companion clapped his hands together. 'I think we just ran out of goblins,' he said.

I looked around. He was right.

'Luckily,' he continued, 'I know where we can find more.'

As if on cue, a group of them trotted past the end of the square. They looked to be heading towards the field.

'Well,' Grams said, 'what are we waiting for?'

I wasn't sure that the clever thing to do was to hunt down more goblins. I suspected that it was to go home, lock the door behind us and close all the curtains. But instead, I found myself heading towards the field with Grams.

'I'm Izzy,' I said to the shaggy man.

He gave me a weird look before his face broke into a grin. My hand disappeared into his as he shook it. 'Nice to meet you Izzy. I'm Wilfred.'

It was my turn to look at him weirdly. The way he had said it, had said his name, was as if to a special person.

One of the others confirmed my suspicion that Wilfred had been taking the piss when he said, 'Leave her alone Will.'

A third man raised his hand and we all stopped. He looked back over his shoulder and put a finger to his lips. Then he gestured that we should spread out. Like that, we slipped into the tree line and crept down towards the field.

If I had been looking forward to my party I would have been devastated when we reached the edge of the trees. Chairs and tables lay smashed in small pieces, and where the dance floor had been erected, now only an area of flattish grass remained. The pieces of the floor were scattered around the grass as if someone very large had played Frisbee with them.

The marquee sagged from its poles in tattered pieces of fabric. My Happy Birthday sign, slashed into two pieces, hung dejectedly from where the opening had been. What had once been beautifully-wrapped presents lay scattered on the ground. Now they resembled the aftermath of Christmas morning, ripped paper and crinkled bows barely covering broken boxes.

But I hardly had time to worry about any of that. A group of my guests had been rounded up and were standing at the far side of the field. A couple of goblins stood guard over them while the rest battled a group of men. They were all dressed in leather and fur.

I looked over at Wilfred. 'You're Border Guards?'

'At your service.' He made a mocking bow.

'What's the plan?' My nerves were starting to kick in. It was one thing to react to being attacked, another thing entirely to stalk and engage a goblin.

'We kill them all.' He laughed maniacally.

Grams looked at me with a wild grin on her face. 'This sure is turning out to be a great party,' she said. 'Although Sabby's going to have your guts for garters when she sees what you've done to that dress.'

I looked down at my shredded, blue dress. It was covered in blood and ripped to the top of my thighs. 'It's far more comfortable like this.'

'Circle around,' one of the Border Guards said. 'We'll hit them from behind.'

'Last one there is a rotten egg.' Grams started to trot in the direction of the fight.

This was crazy. I mean I loved doing things with my Grams: watching movies, making hot chocolate, and toasting marshmallows. But fighting goblins? I didn't think that was in the Grandma/Granddaughter bonding handbook.

Shaking my head, I jogged after her. 'Let's get the guests,' I said. That should hopefully be safer.

We stayed clear of the fighting as we circled around. I could see Grams' wand hand twitching, and I knew she was aching to throw a spell or two into the mix. However, the chaotic mass of men and goblins meant that her spell would as likely hit a Border Guard as a goblin.

My party guests huddled miserably in front of a thick knot of trees. I could see Bobby Helman standing protectively in front of his wife Layla. Blood dribbled from a gash on his arm. The Dickson triplets and Nancy Day and her little girl Betty, were clustered behind them, as if Bobby could protect them all. Two terrifying-looking goblins stood guard, watching us as we approached.

'What are we going to do?' I whispered to Grams. I didn't like my chance of taking on both of them without the element of surprise.

'Watch and learn.' She rubbed her hands together and chuckled. Mumbling something, she flicked her wand at them. I waited for them to start laughing or dancing, but instead, one of them scratched his arm.

Then the other one reached down and scratched his leg. Within the minute they were scratching uncontrollably, their nails leaving lines of blood over their bodies.

'What the?'

Their limbs pulled into their bodies and re-emerged covered in dark fur. Their heads distorted, their noses and mouths pushing away from their eyes, elongating into long snouts.

'Grams…' I started to back away from them.

They snarled as they shrank, their bodies warping as they twisted and moulded. Dropping to all fours, one of them threw back his head and howled.

Two huge, black dogs stood where the goblins had been. Saliva dripped from their massive jaws and red eyes glowed with an evil light. Low growls started in their bellies and worked their way up their throats.

'What did you do?' I gasped as I moved backwards.

'I turned them into guard dogs.'

The growls became more ferocious.

'Why?'

'I must admit, I didn't think that one all the way through,' Grams said, slowly placing one leg behind the other.

Their growls became barks, raw and vicious, as they crept towards us.

'Turn them back,' I said.

'No time,' Grams shrieked. 'Run.'

Their jowls pulled back to expose long fangs as they broke into a charge towards us. There was no way we were going to be able to outrun them.

I screamed as the first dog leapt, gnashing teeth aimed for my throat. Throwing an arm up in front of me, I prayed for a shield. Instead, the dog exploded. Blood spattered like some surreal artwork as chunks of flesh peppered us.

Grams wiped an arm across her face. 'Is that what happened to the watermelon?'

'Kind of.' The watermelon had been more sticky than disgusting.

The second dog circled warily, its hackles raised as it growled and barked. And then Bobby Helman leaped on top of it, wrestling it to the ground. He gripped its jaw shut with both hands as his body pinned it down, and then he ripped its head to the side at an awkward angle. The dog let out a high-pitched yelp as its neck cracked.

Bobby climbed to his feet and wiped his hands on his pants. The dog lay motionless at his feet. 'Thought you could use some help,' he said. He reached back down and picked up one of the daggers the goblins had dropped during the transformation. 'You'll get them to safety?' he asked, pointing at the rest of the group.

'Yes.' I nodded my head.

He gave Layla a quick hug before jogging off to help the Border Guards.

'I could do with a nice cup of tea,' Grams declared. 'Anyone care to join me?'

Nancy stared at Grams with wild eyes. 'A cup of tea?'

'Thirsty work this killing goblins.' Grams pulled her skirts up and started heading back towards the path. After a few seconds Layla and the Dickson Triplets followed.

Betty hugged her arms around her chest and sung softly to herself as she stared around the field. Nancy took her hand and led her after Grams. The little girl continued to sing Happy Birthday as I brought up the rear.

We had reached the top of the path when one of the triplets let out a whimper of fear. It took me a second to hear what they had already; crashing through the trees off to the right of the path. It had to have been caused by more than one person, and I doubted very much that any Border Guard's woodcraft would be so sloppy.

'Go,' I whispered to Grams. 'I'll lead them away.'

The group of women hurried away from the mouth of the path and off towards our house.

I licked my lips and stared toward the noise. Hopefully they would keep going right on past. But of course they didn't, and a few seconds later the first goblin burst from the trees and stared in the direction the women had gone. A quick glance over my shoulder showed me Grams, disappearing from view around the corner. A grotesque smile distorted his face as he pulled his dagger from its sheath.

'Oh no you don't,' I stepped into view. 'Not on my shift.'

Another three goblins emerged from the trees.

Ahh whizbang.

If I just ran off they might decide to go after the easier target Grams had presented. I had to get and hold their attention. I took a deep breath and then sprinted towards them. The lead goblin laughed and moved into a fighting stance. But I had no intention of engaging him.

I leapt up, sailing over their heads as I ran through the air. I had enough time to hope they couldn't see up my skirt before I landed in a crouch. I wasn't sure whether to be pleased or not when the four of them took off after me as I sprinted for the shortcut to the field.

I gained some ground on them as I zigzagged through the trees; their height and bulk made them slow and clumsy. I changed my direction and slowed my pace as the hill became steeper. Trying to maintain my footing and not make any noise took up most of my attention, but I could hear them off to the side. I stopped behind an oak, hugging its vast trunk to stop myself slipping as I peered around its girth.

I could see two shadows moving slowly as they searched for me. Where were the other two?

I was starting to fear that I had misjudged my trajectory when a hand clamped over my mouth. I tried to break away but an arm wrapped around my waist holding me tight. I screamed into the hand and then bit down onto the soft skin.

The hand disappeared as a man swore softly behind me. Eyes open wide, I lifted my sabre and spun towards my attacker. As I turned, a bed of leaves slipped from underneath my feet, sliding down the steep slope. I had a moment to feel surprised as I danced from one foot to the other, trying to regain my balance. My outflung arms clasped that of my attacker and he pulled me to him, but it was too late.

'Your weapon,' a gruff voice said.

I threw the sabre away from me and then we were tumbling down the hill in a jumble of limbs. He cradled me, wrapping his body around mine, but sticks and stones still crashed into me. I buried my face in his chest and held him tight. Finally we slowed, rolling to a stop at the edge of the field.

I opened my eyes and took my first breath since we had started to fall. I lay on my back with him on top of me, my legs entwined through his. He lifted his head and captured my gaze with his midnight-blue eyes. All of a sudden I was totally aware of every inch of his body pressing into mine. I had to remind myself to breathe.

'Aethan.' My voice cracked slightly as I whispered his name.

He lifted a hand towards my face. 'Is that… goblin?' he asked as he pulled a lump of flesh from my cheek.

For a second I had forgotten how I must look. My dress was ruined, my hair a mess and I had blood and gore all over me. 'Possibly,' I said, wriggling to get out from underneath him. This was *not* how I had wanted him to see me.

He held me down for a second longer and I had the absurd thought that he might kiss me. All right, so maybe I *wanted* him to kiss me. But he didn't of course, and I flushed with embarrassment as I clambered to my knees.

There was no chance he would want to court me now after having seen me like this. I felt stupid for thinking that and stupid for caring and stupid for forgetting about the goblins.

And as for those goblins, well, it wasn't possible they *hadn't* heard us sliding down the hill, and Aethan and I had both tossed our weapons. We were defenceless.

He leant down and pulled a dagger from his boot.

Okay, so ***I*** was defenceless. I pushed my hair, which had totally escaped Sabby's ministrations, back behind my ears, wincing at the feel of it; matted with twigs and blood, and I'm sure the occasional piece of goblin.

The lead goblin emerged a few seconds later. The other three weren't far behind. I scanned the ground and picked up a branch, thwacking it against my hands a few times, partly to check it wasn't rotten, but also to make myself feel tougher. It didn't help much.

'Keep moving,' Aethan said to me. 'Don't let them pin you down.'

I had a second to think how weird it was that I felt like we had done this before - it felt very natural to be facing off against the goblins with him by my side, and then they were on us. Aethan danced to the left, slashing his dagger across one of their chests, opening up a trail of blood.

I have to admit that my hands were trembling as I backed across the field. Two of the goblins stalked towards me. One had the dreadlocks that seemed to be common amongst them, but the other had a mowhawk. Both had triumphant sneers on their faces.

A girl and a stick?

I didn't stand a chance.

This wasn't how I had envisioned spending my birthday, but strangely I found I preferred it to the thought of tottering around in those stupid shoes.

I dashed to the side, swinging my branch low at Mowhawk's shins. It wasn't at all what he had been expecting, and the wood had no impediment before it slammed into the tender tissue on top of the bone. He roared and swiped at me with his dagger, but I was already gone.

Dready closed the gap between us and plunged his weapon at my chest. I pivoted to the side, swinging the branch up to deflect his dagger. Hot pain flared in my arm as the tip of his blade sliced through tissue.

I let my momentum carry me around and my branch slammed into the side of his head. He wobbled unsteadily on his feet while he shook his head, his eyes narrowed in anger.

Mowhawk circled around behind me. I threw my stick into the air and cartwheeled forwards, uprighting in time to catch it with one hand.

I heard a grunt and looked over to where Aethan was fighting the other two. One of them was clutching the end of Aethan's dagger where it emerged from his chest. Blood dribbled from his mouth as he sank to his knees. Aethan grabbed the longer weapon from the goblin's hand and then wrenched the second one from its sheath.

'Here,' he said, tossing one of the blades to me.

I grabbed it out of the air and held it up between me and the approaching goblins.

Be a sabre, be a sabre. I stared at it, willing it with all my might. But of course it stayed just as it was. I shook my head in frustration.

Stupid, stupid, stupid.

The goblins spread out, one to each side of me, and then they attacked at the same time. I jumped into the air, wishing I could just stay up there out of their reach, and executed a foreword somersault. I landed so that they were both on the same side of me again. I couldn't let them divide my attention. I had to make them attack me one at a time.

But of course *they* had realised that as well. I danced and jumped and cartwheeled and tumbled, trying to keep them from a double attack. It rankled that my plan was to hold them off long enough for Aethan to dispose of his second goblin. That would mean that he would get three and I, only one.

And then of course there was the ludicrousness of *that* thought. Who cared if he killed more goblins than I did?

He was trading blows with his goblin, throwing in punches and kicks around his blade strikes. He was mesmerising to watch as he flowed across the field. I tore my gaze away from him. I couldn't do with any distractions, or staring at him would be the last thing I did.

It was all very well to stay out of their reach, but I was starting to tire. They were getting closer and closer the slower I got. I parried a blow and swiped at Dready's neck with my blade. He ducked and I caught the top of his head, jarring my wrist as I sliced through to bone. Blood ran freely from the cut, down his forehead and into his eyes. He dashed at it with one hand, growling angrily.

I turned my attention to Mowhawk, but I was too slow. He laughed wickedly as he grabbed my blade arm. I batted at him with the branch in my left hand but he was too close for me to do any real damage. He twisted my wrist till a bone cracked. I screamed in agony, the dagger dropping from my useless fingers.

I kicked him in the shins and tried to pull my arm away but he tightened his grip, pressing his fingers between the broken bits of bone. Red clouded my vision as I fought to stay conscious.

So, this was it.

This was how I was going to die.

I'd had a lot to be thankful for: Mum, Grams and Sabby. I wished I'd had more time with all of them. And well Aethan – I ripped my gaze away from the goblin's feral snarl and looked over at Aethan. I *definitely* wished I'd had some time with him.

He was in the process of finishing off the goblin he was fighting, but it wasn't going to be in time to save me.

I closed my eyes as Mowhawk raised his arm to deliver the killing blow. But it never came. He grunted and then gurgled. I opened my eyes and looked up at him. Blood ran freely down his neck from a wound at his throat.

I yanked out of his grip and staggered back a couple of steps, nursing my wounded hand to my chest. His eyes rolled back in his head and he slumped to the ground.

Meanwhile, Dready was battling a white demon. I hardly recognised Scruffy with his lips drawn back and his hackles up. He leapt and sharp teeth tore a chunk out of Dready's thigh. Blood stained his muzzle pink.

I dropped the branch and picked up the dagger with my left hand. Trying to ignore the pain in my other arm, I stalked the goblin. Distracted by Scruffy he was an easy target. I waited until he kicked out at my familiar and then I drove the blade at the side of his neck.

The aim of my left arm wasn't as true as my right and I missed his neck. Instead, the tip of the dagger drove deep into his ear. The dagger stuck, wedged in the bones of his head, and he fell forwards, dead before he hit the ground.

I had to remember that strike for next time - suddenly sure there *would* be a next time.

Scruffy crossed to my side and sat down, a big smile on his fluffy face as he stared up at me. 'Ruff,' he said.

'Thanks.' I bent down and scratched him behind the ears. I didn't know who looked more disgusting, him or me.

'I think that makes it two to me, one to you and one to your pink dog,' Aethan said as he strode over to us.

I snorted. 'Scruffy and I work as a team. It's two all.'

'That's going to hurt later,' he said, nodding his head at my arm.

'What do you mean, *later?'* A sharp throb was radiating up my arm to my shoulder. It was somewhere between extremely painful and excruciating, but I didn't want to look like a wimp in front of Aethan.

I walked beside him to where the rest of the Border Guard was standing. They had dealt with the remaining goblins while we had been fighting. Wilfred looked over at us and yelled. 'I made ten.'

'Ten?' Aethan said. 'Even Izzy got more than that.'

One of the other men snorted and said, 'Yeah, and she's a girl.'

'I don't mind being beaten by a girl,' Wilfred said, his voice full of fake pompousness, 'as long as it's Isadora.'

Isadora? How did he know my full name?

'Actually,' I said, staring at him (Did I know him?), 'my Grandmother got eleven.'

The men broke out into raucous laughter as Wilfred's face took on a rueful look. One of them clapped his hands together and said, 'Right, back to business.'

Him, I recognised. The long scar running down his face was hard to forget.

He strode over to Aethan. 'How many of ours?' he asked.

It took me a second to realise what he was talking about.

'We lost Backo,' Aethan said, running a hand through his hair. 'And Grant and Steve are pretty badly injured.'

'Civilian casualties?'

'Two down here and one outside the bakery. Poor bastard didn't even see them coming.'

Three? Oh Great Dark Sky, three dead?

Eynsford was a small village; small enough that everybody knew everybody, and now three of us were dead. Anger washed over me, and for a moment I forgot about the pain in my arm.

How dare they? How dare they come here and attack innocent people?

I clenched and unclenched my good fist as the pressure grew inside me. I wanted revenge, I wanted to hunt them all down and make them pay for what they had done. I wanted to find them and rip out their black hearts.

'I want to join the Border Guard.' I was surprised when the words poured out of my mouth.

'Do you now?' The man with the scar gave me a hard look. 'You know you can't wear dresses in the Border Guard.'

'Even better,' I said.

'You have to be eighteen to join.'

I gestured to where the marquee sat slumped on the ground. Crushed presents mingled with table decorations, and my Happy Birthday sign lay trampled into the dirt.

'Happy Birthday,' he said with a totally straight face.

'Come on Rako,' Wilfred yelled from where he was sorting through goblin bodies, 'stop being an arse.'

The very edge of Rako's mouth pulled up slightly. 'Well, okay. But only because we're a little short at the moment.'

I felt the pressure dissipate a little. I wanted blood and I wanted it *now,* but this was better than nothing. At least now I had a chance of exacting revenge.

Scruffy trotted to Rako and sat at his feet. He looked up at him and whined.

'You're a dog,' Rako said.

Scruffy let out a bark and growled. He leapt on a nearby stick and wrestled with it, finally breaking it in two. He looked up at Rako, his tongue hanging out in a doggy grin.

'You're pink,' Rako said. 'We'll be a laughing stock with a pink dog in our ranks.'

Scruffy sat down and started to groom himself. He unfortunately started with his privates. I scooped him up with my good arm and said, 'he'll be white. I promise.'

Rako's lip pulled a little higher. 'I want him fridge-door white.'

'The best I can do is I-had-a-bath-yesterday-but-it-rained-today white.'

Rako snorted. 'It'll do. Enlistment's on Monday at eight.'

He turned and walked to the growing pile of goblin bodies and all of a sudden Aethan and I were alone.

'Sorry 'bout your hand,' I said. He had a red, crescent bruise on the soft tissue between his thumb and first finger. It would have fitted my teeth perfectly.

He looked down at his hand and shrugged. 'That's the least of my worries,' he said.

We stared at each other, an awkward silence ballooning between us. *What worries? Should I say something about the courting thing?*

'I better…' He glanced over to where the rest of the Guard were working.

'Yeah, I better let Mum and Grams know I'm alive.' I was ashamed I hadn't thought of that before. They'd be worried sick by now. Well, Mum would be. Grams would be too busy telling stories to notice I was still gone.

He opened his mouth as if to say something but then just nodded stiffly and trotted over to help Wilfred lift a body.

'If I wasn't confused before,' I said to Scruffy, 'I certainly am now.' I placed him on the ground and headed back to the house.

***

Mum was in a total state when she opened the door. 'Oh thank the Great Dark Sky,' she said, throwing her arms around me.

I gritted my teeth in pain as she pulled me to her. It only lasted a second though before she pushed me away and pointed her finger at me. 'You are in such trouble young lady. I thought you were dead.' Her finger twitched in time with her words.

'I told you she'd be fine,' Grams called from the kitchen.

Mum peered back towards Gram. 'I haven't finished with you,' she said.

Sabby was hovering behind Mum staring at me with her mouth wide open. 'Your hair,' she said. 'Your make-up. Your *dress*. What did you do to that dress?'

I pushed carefully past them. Now that the endorphins were fading my arm was *really* starting to hurt.

'What is that stuff all over you?' she continued.

'Goblin's brains,' Grams called out.

'You don't *know* it was brains,' I said.

The Dickson Twins, Layla, Nancy and Betty were perched on chairs around the table. Layla searched my expression, her face white and pinched.

'Bobby's safe,' I said.

She gasped and sagged backwards, tears of relief falling from her lashes.

'I told you to look after Scruffy,' I said to Mum.

She looked down at my feet and started as if seeing him for the first time. 'But…' She pointed into the kitchen.

A small, white dog lay curled up on Scruffy's bed. His legs moved spasmodically and he whimpered in his sleep.

I looked from my pink familiar to the other one. Scruffy trotted over to the bed and stood next to his counterpart. Light seemed to bend around him and then suddenly, he was gone. The dog on the bed opened his eyes, stretched and shook himself. His coat was tinged the faintest of pinks.

'That is one freaky familiar,' Grams said. 'Cup of tea?'

'I'm thinking healer.' I nodded down at my arm. I had plenty of time to work out Scruffy. But my arm was screaming for attention NOW.

'You're hurt,' Mum said, bustling to my side. 'What happened?'

'I fell.' It was the only answer I could think of that wasn't going to illicit a lecture.

Mum grabbed my wrist and I screeched in pain. 'It's broken,' she said, like I didn't already know that. But I began to cry anyway. It's one thing to be brave in front of a band of Border Guards, it's another thing *entirely* to be brave in front of your own mother.

She deposited me on the couch with a blanket (for the shock) and Sabby came to sit beside me. She placed her wand on my wrist and closed her eyes.

'It's a compound fracture,' she said. 'We'll have to get Mum to heal it.'

Grindella was a healer at the Eynsford Hospital.

'She'll be busy.' I had a feeling there might be a lot of people in Eynsford in need of a healer.

'I'll make you a special pot of tea,' Grams said, bustling around the kitchen. 'It'll help with the pain till she gets here.'

I drank the tea and slumped on the couch with Sabby holding my good hand, and Scruffy curled up by my side. The pain slowly ebbed away to a dull ache.

'I'm worried about Thomas.' I was starting to slur my words.

'Who?'

'My friend from fencing.' I was hoping that he hadn't been the 'poor bastard' outside the bakery. He had a real penchant for their custard tarts.

'Oh,' Sabby said, 'the human.' It wasn't humans Sabby had a problem with. I wasn't sure why, but she didn't have much time for Thomas.

I gave her a level look and she shrugged one shoulder. Which of her two heads was the real one?

She pulled a face. 'I'm sure he's safe.'

'I nearly wasn't,' I slurred. 'A goblin did this.' I raised my arm and then giggled. It didn't feel like it was attached to my body any more. 'What is in this tea?' I started to laugh.

'What do you mean a goblin did this?' Mum was suddenly right beside me.

I peered up at her. Why was her mouth above her eyes? 'He was going to slit my throat.' I had to concentrate on every word. 'But Scruffy saved me.'

'Isadora Scrumpleton, if you ever pull a stunt like this again.'

Pretty lights, spinning round.

'I'm going to join the Border Guard.' I knew the words were coming out of me but they sounded like they were echoing from the other side of the room.

Dizzy, dizzy, dizzy…

Noise was coming out of Mum's mouth. I stared up at her, trying to work out what she was saying. But the pretty lights grew brighter and brighter, flashing and dancing before my eyes, and then the dizzy, dizzy, dizzy claimed me for its own.

Chapter Six

Memories

When I finally woke the next morning my arm was bandaged and hanging in a sling over my chest. I wiggled it experimentally. There was slight pain at the extreme ranges of motion, but apart from that it was fine. I was glad I had passed out *before* they had healed me.

When I finally summoned up the courage to venture downstairs (I seemed to remember telling Mum I was joining the Border Guard), there were two men sitting at the kitchen table. One of them I recognised, Radismus Pringle, the other I didn't, but by the shape of his ears I assumed he was a faery.

Mum was in the kitchen whipping up what appeared to be lemon cake. She was taking magical short cuts and it was in the final stages of cooking.

I hovered in the doorway trying to ascertain how much trouble I was in. She glanced up and gave me a small, tight smile.

'Scruffy?' I asked.

'Already fed him.'

'I swear he just came downstairs with me.'

'Been here the whole time.' Her face was expressionless. 'Isadora, these gentlemen have come to offer their help in your training. You already know Radismus of course, but you haven't met Wolfgang Periwinkle yet.'

I nodded my head at Radismus and then held my hand out to Wolfgang. He took it gently in his and stared into my eyes, fixing me with his gaze. A surge of power trickled through me and then he broke eye contact and it was gone. I took a step backwards, blinking rapidly.

'What was that?' I asked.

'I'm sorry my dear,' he said in a soft, melodic voice. 'I suppose I should have pre-warned you, but I didn't want to give you the chance to put any barriers in place. I needed to see your mind as it is normally.'

'You can look into my mind?'

'It is a talent peculiar to my family. It is why we have always been trainers to the Royal family.'

'Oh.' I wasn't exactly sure what he meant.

'Can you explain what's going on when she sleeps?' my mother asked.

Wolfgang leant towards me, his large, grey eyes were solemn. 'You've been dream-walking?'

'I don't dream,' I said, 'so I don't see how I've been dream-walking.'

'You dream,' he said, nodding his head. 'But your faery powers and your witch powers are at odds with each other. Only the faery part of you is dream-walking. Because you identify as a witch, when you are awake, you are unaware of what has happened.'

'So...' I was having trouble getting my head around that, 'because I *think* I'm a witch, I don't know what my faery part is up to?'

'That is a simplistic version,' he said, sitting back in his seat, 'but for our purposes it will do nicely.'

'Will that change?' If I'd been making out with Aethan I wasn't sure if I wanted to remember it. I got all squirmy and twitchy just thinking about it.

'It should, if we are able to reconcile your powers. Radismus and I will be working together to attempt this.'

'Is it dangerous?' I asked.

'The procedure Radismus and I will be...'

'No, no,' I cut him off. 'Dream-walking. Is it dangerous?'

He stared at me for a second before answering. 'When an injury occurs during dream-walking, the physical manifestation appears on the body of the walker.'

'So that's a yes,' I said.

'If, for argument's sake, you were to encounter something terrifying in your dreams and suffer wounds as a consequence, then the emotional ramifications of this would transfer those wounds to your sleeping body.'

'So if I were to say...,' I paused not sure I really wanted to know the answer.

'If you were to die during your dream-walk then yes, you would never awaken,' Wolfgang correctly answered my unasked question.

Buzznuckle. Here I was flouncing around at night doing something I had absolutely no conscious control over and now I find out it could be deadly. That sucked big time.

The oven chimed, announcing the imminent arrival of the lemon cake. I could hear Mum removing plates from the cupboard as I contemplated Wolfgang's words. I really had to get a grip on my faery side.

'So, umm,' I said once Mum had returned with the cake, 'how are we going to do this training?'

Radismus reached for a piece. 'Wolfgang and I will work with you to assimilate the two parts of your personality.'

Hmmmphf. He made it sound like I was schizophrenic. 'When do we start?'

Wolfgang chuckled. 'As soon as we finish your mother's delicious-smelling cake.

An hour later, I was sitting cross-legged on the floor with Radismus and Wolfgang. We were linked in a circle with our eyes closed, concentrating on our breathing.

'Now move deeper,' Wolfgang said, his voice hypnotic and soothing.

I felt myself drift away from my body.

'No Izzy, deeper *into* yourself.'

I stopped my movement and concentrated instead on the black depth of my core. I moved slowly down the dark tunnel. The walls were soft, muffling all exterior sound. Soon I floated at the centre of my being, cocooned in the darkness like a child in a womb.

'Radismus, you and I are going to try to reach each other through Izzy,' Wolfgang said.

'Huh?' I could feel myself start to move back up the tunnel away from my centre. 'Is that going to hurt?'

'Relax Izzy,' he said. 'It won't hurt at all.'

'So Wolfgang,' said Radismus from my other side, 'what are we trying to achieve?'

'We are going to try to unite Isadora's two sides. You will naturally be drawn to her witch side and will work your way through that part of her conscious. I will come through the faery side. If we are able to complete our joining in the heart of her, her two sides will flow together and become one.'

'Ahhh,' I said, 'as you work your way through my conscious sides are you going to be able to read my mind?'

'No Izzy, your memories are safe.'

I relaxed at the news. Fantastic, the two of them were going to do their stuff and pretty soon I was going to remember everything. I was nervous about the remembering. What if it were like watching a movie - seeing but not feeling?

'All righty,' I finally said. Either way I wanted to get it over and done with. 'Let's get started.'

I tried to relax as they began, but the sensation of their minds entering mine resulted in a tickling sensation around the edges of my head. I giggled and started to pull away.

'Izzy,' said Wolfgang, 'if we de-link now it will take ages to get back to this point.'

'Sorry,' I said. 'It tickles.'

'The sensation will stop as soon as we are in.'

True to his word, a couple of minutes later the tickling stopped and, instead, warmth flowed across my mind in a gentle wave. I relaxed into the sensation, stilling my thoughts which had been jumping randomly around inside my head. (Aethan, goblins, Scruffy, Aethan, Border Guards had pretty much been the order of them.) As my thoughts mellowed, the warmth sped up its progress, melting further into me.

'That's better Izzy,' Wolfgang said.

Both sides of my head were warm and buzzing with energy. 'Have you done it?

'Not yet,' Radismus grunted.

'What's wrong?'

'You are putting up some resistance,' Wolfgang said.

I could feel pushing and prodding deep inside me.

'I've never done anything like this before,' Radismus said to Wolfgang. 'Is this barrier normal?'

'No,' Wolfgang replied.

'It's like a thick, latex layer.'

'Try tearing at it,' Wolfgang advised.

'Please don't break me.' The pushing sensation changed to a pulling one.

'What is that bright light on your side?' Radismus asked.

'That's Izzy's power.'

'But… it's so bright.' There was wonder in Radismus's voice.

'Faery powers look different to witch powers, but even for a faery she is strong.'

Was that what I had felt the first time I had touched my power? The never-ending tide of energy I had dipped into?

'What's your side look like?' Wolfgang asked Radismus.

'Hmmmm. Pretty standard for a witch, except there are glowing patches, pulsing with energy.'

'Don't touch those,' Wolfgang advised. 'That's faery energy soaked through to her witch side. Most unusual.' His tone was analytical.

'So what will that mean?' I asked.

'That your faery powers will have dominance, but we've already seen signs of that.'

'We have?'

'Your control over air.'

'My what?'

'Your shields are hardened air.'

'Oh.' I thought about all of that and then something else occurred to me. 'Does this have something to do with Scruffy?'

'What about Scruffy?'

I told him about Scruffy's collar and about how last night we had all seen two of him.

Wolfgang started chuckling. 'The familiar chooses the witch and forms a bond with them. This happens because they are similar.'

'Are you saying I'm a dog?'

'No. I am saying that you are loyal, intelligent and affectionate. The character traits of the familiar and the witch they choose are similar.'

'Oh.' Phantom certainly shared character traits with Sabby. They were both proud, majestic and easily offended. But then they were fiercely loyal to the small number of people they let into their circle. 'That doesn't explain the things that keep happening.'

'You are unique Isadora. A witch with your talents has probably never been born before.'

I let out an involuntary laugh. *Me? The most powerful witch ever born?* It was so funny it was ridiculous.

'So you think Scruffy has his own powers?' I said once I had stopped laughing.

'I think where you are concerned, anything is possible.'

'What about the fact that he seems to be able to be in two places at once?'

'At a guess I would say that Scruffy is manifesting your breach in your psyche in his own way. He also has two halves. While one is upstairs with you the other is down in the kitchen with your mother.'

'That's plain weird,' I said.

'I don't think I can go on much longer,' Radismus said.

'Dear fellow,' Wolfgang replied in a worried voice, 'if you are tired you must get out before Izzy's consciousness swamps you.'

'I seem to be stuck to this barrier.'

'Pull yourself away from it.'

'I can't.' Radismus's voice was weaker.

I wasn't sure what was going to happen if my consciousness swamped him, and I didn't want to find out. 'You can do it,' I said.

'I can see you,' Wolfgang told him, 'your hands are twisted in the barrier. Turn them anticlockwise and pull hard.'

There was a moment of silence during which I felt tugging, and then with one last wrench he was free. Before I could feel relief, he let out a cry.

'Not the golden patch,' Wolfgang yelled.

For a second I felt him, I knew him; his every thought of terror and wonderment blazed through my mind. Wolfgang yelled out as Radismus let go of our hands and slumped to the floor. I opened my eyes; saw the paleness of his cheeks, the pallid cast of his face and dived deep inside myself. I swam back towards the cavernous darkness until I found a softly glowing patch and, grabbing hold of its edges, I pulled myself through.

***

I stood in a flower-filled meadow, edged on one side by the creek and the other by the forest. Radismus was nowhere to be seen.

What if he had ended up in another part of my mind? How were we going to get out?

I decided to concentrate on the *finding* part of the problem first and deal with the *getting out* part later.

I scratched a reference line on the ground and then started walking along the sweeping curve of the river bed. I had only been travelling for a few minutes when I saw a shadowy figure in the distance. I quickened my pace, hoping Radismus was there.

A small girl sang to herself while she picked a posy of flowers. She had long, black hair, and, when she glanced up, I realised with a start that it was a younger version of me.

She looked right through me, as if I weren't there, and continued breaking off flowers.

'Well that answers that question.' Radismus slid out from behind a tree and walked towards me. 'I didn't want to scare her.'

'You're okay?' I resisted my urge to hug him.

The little girl looked up again. This time she glanced back over her shoulder. Standing slowly, she turned around. Her eyes widened and she backed up a few steps.

A monster slurched from the edge of the forest. Easily a dozen limbs dangled from its slug-like body, none of them were legs. A large mouth dominated its head, rows of sharp teeth visible through the drooling saliva.

The flowers fell from the little girl's fingers as her mouth opened wide in a scream.

'Run,' I said, backing away from it. 'Run.'

The creature let out a high-pitched mewl that made the hair on the back of my neck stand on end, and slithered towards us. The little girl turned and fled across the field. Radismus and I took off after her.

Even though we were all running as fast as we could (you don't keep anything in reserve when something from a nightmare is chasing you), a quick glance over my shoulder showed it was gaining. We weren't going to be able to outrun it, but there was nothing to use as a weapon.

And then a horse emerged over the top of a low rise, galloping at an angle towards us. A young man sat astride the horse, his sword drawn. They were moving faster than the monster but I wasn't sure if they would make it in time.

The monster let out another cry and the little girl's legs slowed. It called again and she stopped and turned to face it.

'Run,' I yelled, but I could feel it too. It was calling us, willing us to stop.

The horse ran as fast as it could, its head out straight in front of its body as its hooves flew over the ground.

'I'm coming,' the man yelled.

I forgot all about the monster as my eyes flew to his face. Aethan. Here. Coming to save us.

The monster let out a shrill cry as it reached out its multiple arms to grasp the girl. Its mouth opened wider and wider, till it seemed it would swallow her whole.

Young Aethan sheathed his sword and leant forward in his saddle, reaching a hand down to my adolescent self. At full gallop he grabbed her arm, the force whipping her up and around behind him, out of the arms of the monster.

The girl wrapped her arms around Aethan's waist as they galloped off.

The monster was right behind us as Radismus and I ran after him.

'Wait,' I called out. 'Help.'

A look over my shoulder showed me it almost had us. I screamed in rage and frustration and turned to face it. I might have no weapon, but I wasn't going down without a fight.

I could hear Radismus panting as he stood beside me. It was on us before I could formulate a plan, flowing over us, through us, beyond us. It kept slithering in the direction Aethan had disappeared.

I slumped to the ground and rolled onto my back. 'Oh Dark Sky,' I said. 'I thought it had us.'

'It was a memory,' Radismus said, flopping down beside me. 'Your memory.'

'You'd think I'd remember *that*.'

We lay there till our heart beats calmed and then we climbed back to our feet.

'We need to get out of here,' Radismus said.

'Any ideas?' I mean I know it was my mind we were in, but *he* was the teacher.

'Let's keep walking down the river.'

We made our way back to the river and continued the direction I had been walking. After a while, the landscape changed from wildflower-dotted fields to hard, rocky outcrops.

An older version of me than the last one, lay on the river-side of the rocks. She was peering through two large boulders. A couple of Border Guards stood not far from where she hid. They finished their conversation and then one of them turned and ran off into the trees. The other waited till he was gone before turning towards the boulders. It was Aethan.

'I know you're there,' he said, 'so you may as well come out.'

The girl had a disgruntled look on her face as she stood up. 'I didn't make any noise,' she said. 'I did it just as you showed me.'

'It's not a good idea to wear perfume when you are stalking someone,' he said.

She blushed and looked at her feet. 'But apart from that?'

'Apart from that I wouldn't have known you were there.'

Appeased, she smiled at him. 'Will you teach me to use a sword?'

'You shouldn't even be here.'

'You taught me to hunt.'

'That's different.'

'How do you expect me to defend myself?'

He stared at her for a moment and then shook his head. 'It's dangerous for you here.'

'Hence the sword lessons.'

'I tell you what,' his sudden smile lit up his face, 'if you can watch me for a whole night without me knowing you are there, I'll teach you.'

'One whole night?' she clarified.

'One whole night.'

'Well then, you had better start teaching me.'

'I knew you were here.'

'Ahhh,' her smug smile threatened to split her face in two, 'but you didn't know I was there last night.'

'Last night?' His eyebrows rode up his brow.

'When you and that blonde girl were doing *interesting* things with your mouths.' I knew my voice well enough to know that she hadn't been at all thrilled about it.

He flushed as he looked at her. 'You were there?'

'Ahuh. So pay up.'

He shook his head. 'Insufferable youngling.'

'A deal's a deal.'

'All right.' He didn't seem too pleased about it. 'Be here tomorrow night and we'll start.'

They shimmered and faded from view.

'Huh,' I said. *A blonde?* How many years ago had that been?

'We'd better keep going.' Radismus turned back towards the river.

He liked blondes?

I followed after Radismus, walking in silence.

Who was she? Was she still in the picture?

A line drawn in the dirt of the riverbank broke me from my obsessive contemplation of the blonde. The scenery around us had changed, but I was pretty sure that that was the line I had drawn.

'What's wrong,' Radismus asked.

'I drew this line when I first got here.' I pointed at it.

'Ahhhh.' Radismus stared at the line for a few moments. 'Well I guess we're not going to get out of here by walking,' he finally replied.

'I guess not.' I jumped into the sky as high as I could with my arms stretched out.

'What are you doing?' Radismus asked after my third attempt.

'This is where I came through. I thought maybe I'd be able to jump out.'

'Even if you could Izzy, I could never jump that high.'

'Well it doesn't seem to be working,' I said. 'Let's keep walking while we think about it.

We continued down the river until we stumbled across another mini-movie of Aethan and me.

We were both holding wooden swords. 'That's better,' Aethan said. 'Now move your feet a little further apart.'

I shuffled my feet till they were shoulder width apart.

'Does that feel more comfortable?'

'It feels more stable,' I said.

'Right, so let's begin.'

'Wait,' I said. 'That's it? You're just going to attack me?'

'What better way to learn?'

They faded from view and we continued walking.

'So this is where you spend your nights?' Radismus asked.

'Guess so.'

'Still don't remember?'

'I was hoping I would if you and Wolfgang were successful today.'

A few minutes later we came to the mark I had made.

'We must be going in circles.' Radismus sat next to the river and trailed his fingers in the water.

'It would appear so.' I tossed a blade of grass onto the surface and watched as it disappeared into the distance.

'Radismus,' I said.

'Yes Izzy.'

'How deep do you think this river is?'

He picked up a small stone and threw it into the water. We could see it disappear below the surface, heading towards the bottom.

'Deep,' he replied. 'What are you thinking?'

'I'm thinking we go for a swim.'

He clambered to his feet and stared at the river. 'Okay,' he finally said.

I held out my hand. 'Don't let go.'

He grasped it tightly and looked at me. 'On the count of three?'

Nodding my head I said, 'One.'

'Two,' he continued.

'Three,' we both shrieked and, holding tight to each other's hand, we jumped into the deep, cold waters of my mind.

***

The river was powerful. I clutched Radismus's hand as it swept us up in its current, and tumbled us with its turbulence.

Floating easily, we raced along the riverbank. Rocks gave way to forest, which in turn gave way to wild-flower dotted plains. Just when I was beginning to think we were travelling a loop, Radismus squeezed my hand.

The water, previously a dark blue, was starting to lighten. The way ahead was brighter, the water warmer. Perhaps it was time to get out. I started to swim to the side, but now the riverbanks were gone. Water stretched as far as I could see.

The light blazed brilliant, like a volcanic explosion, and a wall of fire appeared before us. I heard Radismus scream as we raced towards it.

The water glowed and boiled, bubbling against my skin. The fire reared into the sky before us. I shut my eyes as the merciless river swept us through.

One second of blazing agony as the fire flashed over my skin, then the pain was gone. All that was left was a tingling sensation. Effervescence swaddled me.

I felt Radismus spasm, his grip on my hand loosening as his body convulsed. And then he was gone. I tried to contain my panic as I searched for him.

The tingling on my skin was a distraction. It danced and twirled along my nerve endings, causing me to quiver and shiver. It soothed me and stimulated me at the same time, sending tendrils of power thrilling through me. It swirled around me and within me, glorious, divine; both strange and familiar. And that was when I realised, I was bathing in my power.

I whirled faster and faster through the brilliant vortex, tumbling and turning, until finally the river burst, like a raging torrent over a dam wall, and I fell and I fell and I fell…

Chapter Seven

Queen Of Awkward

The first thing I saw when I opened my eyes was Wolfgang's worried face peering into mine.

'You're all right?' he queried.

I nodded. 'Radismus?'

'I'm fine,' Radismus said from behind me.

'You disappeared when the river swept us through the fire.'

'I regained consciousness.'

'You entered the water?' Wolfgang asked him.

'It was the only thing we could do to get out. We were lost in Izzy's memories.'

Looking thoughtful, Wolfgang sat back on his haunches. 'You touched her power?' he finally asked.

'Briefly,' Radismus replied.

'What does that mean?' I asked.

'I'm not sure,' Wolfgang said. 'What's done is done and only time will tell.' He looked at the clock on the loungeroom wall. 'Speaking of time, the Prince will be here soon.'

'Pardon?'

'Ahh. Silly me. I seem to have forgotten to mention it. Prince Aethan has requested the pleasure of your company.'

'He's coming here? To see me?' I leapt off the floor and dashed for my room. Aethan was coming. Here. Soon. And I had nothing to wear.

Part of me was a little pissed, what with him just 'requesting my company' and all that. It would have been nice to be asked if I were free. What if I'd had plans?

Ahhh – who was I kidding? If I'd had plans I would have cancelled them.

I raced straight to the mirror hoping Sabby was in her bedroom. I pictured her mirror, where it hung over her dressing table and then I willed myself into it.

'Help,' I shrieked.

'Izzy?' Parts of her face became visible. I could see an eye, half her nose and part of her mouth. 'You broke my mirror. How did you break my mirror?'

'I have an emergency.' I broke her mirror? Dark Sky, I couldn't even make a simple spell work the way it was meant to.

'Did you use your wand?'

'It doesn't make any difference.' I was useless with or without my wand.

'Hang on.' She mumbled under her breath and flicked her wand and suddenly I could see all of her face. 'What's wrong?'

'Aethan's coming and I don't know what to wear.'

'So you need to know what the proper clothing etiquette for a witch courting a Fae Prince is?'

'Yes.'

'Hang on and I'll consult the Witch/Faery Courting Handbook.'

'There's a handbook for that?'

'I was being facetious.'

'Not helping.'

'Wear something nice.'

I heard the front doorbell ring. 'Here's here. Oh Great Dark Sky he's here.'

'Huh.'

'What?'

'I would have liked to have been there, that's all.'

'Next time. I promise. Gotta go.' I let her end the communication spell.

Mum came up the stairs and started ferreting around in my wardrobe. 'Here.' She passed me a long, flowing dress.

'Not too much for this time of day?'

'Oh, I don't think so.' She glanced back down the stairs.

'Oh no. What's he wearing?'

'It's not so much him. It's his entourage.'

'Entourage?' My voice shot up an octave and sweat broke out on my forehead.

'Well, you know how I said courting him would be similar to dating?'

'Yes.'

'I was half right.'

I sat on the edge of my bed and put my head between my knees. 'Can you tell them my arm's too sore?'

'You don't need to do this. Just say the word and I'll tell them all to go away.'

I was *so* tempted to say the word. But then I remembered the feel of his body pressing into mine. And although *that* thought didn't help at all with the nerves, it did make me think that perhaps this might be worth it.

I stood up and pulled the dress over my head. Then I checked my hair. It was clean, which was about all I could say for it, but considering the state of it the last time he had seen me it would do. 'Let's go.'

Mum nodded and led me back down the stairs.

'Where's Grams?' I couldn't believe she would miss a shindig like this.

'Haven't seen her all morning.'

I sighed. One less on my team.

Wolfgang was waiting for us at the foot of the stairs. He took Mum's hand and said, 'Prunella Babcock, I have the great pleasure of introducing you to Prince Aethan Gabrielle.' He swept his hand gracefully toward Aethan.

I had a sudden urge to bolt out the back door, through the paddock and all the way across the country, but then Aethan moved into my view and I decided I might stay.

He wasn't wearing his normal fur and leather (which was lucky, because they revealed *way* too much muscle to allow my brain and my mouth to co-ordinate) but he looked every bit as devastating. A cream shirt, open at the neck and tucked into dark pants, was partly covered by an ermine-trimmed cape. His dark hair looked wild and rumpled and I wondered if it felt as silky as it looked. But it was his eyes that captivated me the most. Midnight blue, they captured mine while I struggled to remember how to breathe.

He released me from his gaze, sweeping Mum's hand up in his and bowing his head. 'Ms Babcock,' he said in his rich voice, 'I ask your formal permission to court your daughter Isadora.'

Mum bowed to him and in a stiff voice said, 'Prince Aethan, I give you my formal permission to court my daughter Isadora. Please may I present her to you?' I gather that Wolfgang had been giving her etiquette lessons while I had been upstairs freaking out.

Then they both turned to look at me. 'Isadora,' said Mum in that stilted voice, 'may I present Aethan Gabrielle, Prince and second heir to the throne of the Kingdom of Isilvitania.' She really wasn't helping with my nerve issues.

And then I realised that I seemed to be the only one there who didn't know their lines.

Ah buzznuckle.

Mum took my hand and placed it in Aethan's.

'Hi.' My stomach was tap dancing and my heart was keeping time. I didn't know where to look or what to say. I wanted to be as close to him as possible and as far away at the same time. It was uncomfortable, to say the least, and I didn't know how I was going to behave normally.

Queen Eloise saved me from the excruciating moment. She strode through the front door and said, 'Shall we retire to the garden?' I hadn't realised till that moment that a group of faeries was clustered outside the door.

'Oh, ummm, sure,' I mumbled.

Aethan offered me his arm and we headed for the path to the field. A quick peep over my shoulder revealed that everybody was following us.

'Seriously,' I said to Aethan, 'they're all going with us?'

'I'm afraid so,' he said. 'All part of the courtship deal. They are assuring that I do not ruin your virtue.'

I felt my cheeks erupt into flame. *Ruin my virtue?* I had a feeling I might enjoy that.

Had we been doing 'interesting things' with *our* lips?

'So do we… at night…' I squirmed in embarrassment.

'You really don't remember anything?'

I shook my head, risking a quick glance up at him.

He looked down at my glowing face and grinned. 'It's nice having you on the back foot for once.'

I narrowed my eyes as I stared at him.

'Normally I can't shut you up.'

I wasn't sure if talking-too-much was such a great attribute, but he didn't seem to notice my wince.

The field opened up before us. Someone, I'm guessing it was the faeries, had decorated the meadow. Ribbons and bells moved in the breeze, twirling and tinkling gently. Brightly coloured pavilions made of the softest silk had been erected over rugs littered with cushions and small tables.

'I hope you don't mind,' Aethan said. 'After yesterday I wasn't sure if it were appropriate.'

I glanced around. 'You're expecting another attack?'

'No. I mean using this space for merriment, so soon.'

'I think it better that we embrace life and not let evil dictate what we do.'

'Touché.' He took me by the hand and helped me lower myself to a cushion. Scruffy immediately burrowed into a pillow on my right, turning around a few times before collapsing onto his back with his legs in the air.

The crowd dispersed evenly around us and a rumble of conversation started. At least they weren't all staring and waiting to see what we would do. I didn't think I would survive that.

I cleared my throat and looked back at Aethan. 'So here we are.' I tapped my hand on one of the pillows and looked back out to the field. I was officially the Queen of Awkward.

'I wish I could help you remember,' he said, 'it would make this all so much easier.'

'You said that,' I sat up straighter and leant toward him, 'when your mother came to the house. You told me things would be easier if I could remember. What do you mean?'

He stared at me for a few beats and then glanced down as he plucked a blade of grass. 'I can't tell you.'

'Why?'

He lowered his voice. 'There are things that will become known to you once you join the Border Guard. Until then I cannot mention them.'

'Once I join?'

'Once you have sworn your oaths you will be told.'

'But,' I said, 'I already know.' It was a long shot. 'When we are together at night, I already know.'

'You guessed some of it, but there are still things you don't know.'

I slumped back into my cushion. It was only one day till I signed up, I could wait till then.

A Fae woman stepped gracefully into the space in front of us. With her long, swan neck and her full lips and cheekbones, she was so beautiful I felt deflated in comparison. 'Pray Aethan, do tell us how you met this adorable creature.' She fluttered her long lashes at me.

'Izzy, this is my elder sister, Isla.' He didn't seem very happy about her intrusion.

'I am sure there will be plenty of time to get to know each other, but for now I want to know how you met.' She was even prettier when she pouted.

'Don't ask *me,*' I said. I was pretty sure I knew, but was looking forward to hearing Aethan's interpretation of the event.

He pressed his lips together and then let out a small sigh. 'We met about six months ago.'

'Yes but where?' She pressed her hands together and leaned toward us.

'Isadora stumbled into my dream.' He looked at me. 'It's common amongst untrained dream-walkers.'

'Details please.' The look in her eyes belied the sing-song quality of her voice.

'We started talking and that was pretty much that.'

I knew we'd met earlier than that. Was it the lie that caused the tension around his eyes or his sister's interest in the subject?

'Oh Aethan.' She threw back her head and tinkled out a laugh. 'You're so unromantic. Isadora you will have to teach him how to write love letters and pretty poetry.' She leant over and ran a hand down the side of my cheek. 'Such a lovely face. He shouldn't have trouble finding things to write about.'

Still laughing, she stood and made her way to Queen Eloise. She bent low, her voice a murmur as she whispered in her mother's ear. Queen Eloise let out a laugh and clapped her hands. 'What a good idea,' she said.

I felt Aethan stiffen at my side as she rose to her feet. 'Isla has had the most ravishing idea,' she said to the group of faeries. 'When next we come, Aethan is to read us a poem. A love poem, written for Isadora.'

I cringed back into the cushion. Oh Great Dark Sky. A love poem? I could feel myself starting to spontaneously combust at the mere thought of it. How was I going to handle him reading me a love poem? I groaned as I remembered I had promised Sabby she could come next time. I was *never* going to hear the end of it.

A look at Aethan's face showed the horror I was sure was on mine.

Hmmmphf. It was one thing for *me* to be embarrassed by the thought of him writing me a love poem; it was another thing entirely for *him* to be.

As I cleared my throat and opened my mouth to say something, anything to change the subject, Queen Eloise clapped her hands again. 'It is time for us to depart. Aethan, say your goodbyes.'

He helped me to my feet and then bowed low over the hand he still held. 'Till next time.'

His lips scorched the back of my hand as they touched my skin. I found myself wondering what they would do to my neck. Thoughts like that did nothing to quell the fire which had set up camp on my cheeks again.

He joined the group of faeries and I watched as they took a couple of steps before disappearing from view. 'Neat party trick,' I said to Scruffy.

'One that you will no doubt learn,' Mum said as she came to stand by my side.

As we walked back to the house it wasn't their method of travel I thought about and it wasn't the conversation with Isla or the thought of the humiliating poem. I wondered what it was like meeting him at night when there was nobody else to see. I shivered as I thought about the feel of his lips on my skin and I hoped I would remember soon.

Chapter Eight

Bada Bing Bada Boom!

I wasn't sure what I was more nervous about; the fact that in an hour and a half I would be joining the Border Guard, or the fact that Mum still hadn't said anything about it. It was also the first time that I wouldn't be living under Eric's roof. I hadn't realised how much comfort I had taken from his protection.

I was buttering my toast, trying to ignore the butterflies flying lazy loops around my belly, when there was a knock on the door. I opened it to find Sabina and Thomas shoving each other.

'I was here first,' Sabby said, pushing past Tom.

'Heard you were going, thought I'd say bye.' Tom stopped to scratch Scruffy behind the ears before helping himself to my toast. I sighed and put two more pieces of bread in the toaster.

Sabina picked up the Border Guard brochure I had strategically placed on the table. Mum often needed an opening to berate me, and it was better to let her get it out of her system than let it build any further.

'I can't believe you're doing it,' Sabby said.

'Yeah, I can't believe you're doing it.' Where Sabby's voice had been filled with horror, Thomas's was tight with excitement.

'Yep.' My casualness belied the nerves I felt at what I was about to do.

'I thought it was the tea talking.' Sabina sighed and took a seat at the table.

Mum clanged a pot into the sink and started scrubbing it viciously.

'Signing up to be a protector of the people, that's a big deal.' Thomas took a seat next to Sabby. 'Guarding the borders between our lands and the Fae, fighting orcs and goblins.'

Mum opened a cupboard and threw the pot into the back corner.

'It's a noble occupation. I only wish I had the guts to do it.'

'And the ability to see blood without fainting,' Sabby said.

Thomas ignored her and continued. 'There's all that mystery surrounding the Guards though. I wonder if the rumours are true?'

I could hear Mum mumbling as she thumped a bowl onto the table and poured some flour into it.

'About them eating babies?' I was pretty sure *that* wasn't true. And if it was, I was quitting.

'No, about them being a secret cult.'

I hadn't heard the secret cult rumours. 'Well I'll know soon enough.'

'Yes.' He picked up another piece of toast. 'But you won't be able to tell us.'

If what Aethan had said were true, that was probably closer to the truth than what Tom really thought.

Three eggs flew from the open fridge towards the bowl. Two made it into the flour mixture; the other smashed into the side of the bench and slid to the floor. Scruffy leapt up and raced to the mess, swallowing the egg, shell and all, in one gulp.

'I don't know why you're bothering,' Sabby said.

'What do you mean?'

'You and Aethan are going to get married and live happily-ever-after in his big castle.'

'Married?' *Geez.* I'd spent, what, all of an hour with the guy, and Sabby was talking marriage.

'Where's your grandmother?' I wasn't sure if Thomas changed the subject because he was uncomfortable with it, or if he could see that ***I*** was.

'Not sure.' I had been wondering the same thing. It wasn't like Grams to not be here to say goodbye.

Mum snarled something that sounded like, 'Death wish,' and chucked the mixing bowl at the sink. It missed, bouncing off the splashback and spinning on its edge before settling onto its side.

'Mum,' I said, 'you'll break it.' I knew she could mend it afterwards but that wasn't the point. My going was.

'Oh, so you care about me breaking *that*,' she snapped.

Oh boy. Here we go.

'What about my heart? Do you care about breaking my heart?' Most of the time Mum was the picture of sensibility, but occasionally she gave Grams and Sabina a run for the Drama-Queen-of-the-Year title.

'How am I breaking your heart?'

'By, by,' she waved her hands around in the air, 'going off to die.'

I let out a big breath of air. 'Mother, I am not going off to die. I'm going to learn how to defend myself.'

'But why? What did I do wrong?'

I glanced at the clock. If I didn't leave soon I would be late, and I *really* didn't want to be late.

'Oh Mother.' I pushed back my seat and went to hug her. 'You didn't do anything wrong.'

'She's always been a freak,' Sabby said.

The corners of Mum's mouth quirked up at the corners, but tears rolled down her face.

'I'll be safe,' I said. And if I weren't, well I just wouldn't tell her. 'I'll talk to you tonight, I promise, but I have to go.'

She hugged me fiercely and then wiped her eyes with the back of her hands. Mum's tantrums never lasted long. 'Tonight,' she said.

'*You* may want to instigate that,' Sabby said, as I carried my bag to the back door. 'She broke my mirror the other day.'

I poked my tongue out at her while I waited for Tom to pull the door open for me. I had already packed Scruffy's bed and it only took me a moment to squeeze my bag into my small boot.

Excitement, anxiety and nerves were all mixing together and I was starting to feel nauseous. The prolonged farewell was not helping the situation and there was nothing to be done but get on with it. I started the car and pulled out of the driveway, and, with one final wave, I set off for London and my new life.

***

I had worked myself into quite a state by the time I reached the Barracks. The whole I'm-going-off-to-join-the-Border-Guard thing had been a lot easier whilst eating toast in my kitchen. Now that I was there, driving past groups of men training in the fields, I wasn't so sure about the idea.

What if I made an idiot of myself? What if I wasn't good enough? What if Mum was right and I died?

Eeeek.

If I kept thinking those sorts of things I'd turn tail and flee. Instead I concentrated on the anger I'd felt the other day. I wanted to help keep our land safe, I wanted to stop the senseless violence. And, if I were totally honest, a deep, dark part of me wanted revenge.

About a dozen young men stood at the front of the barracks, waiting in line to give their name to the huge, hairy Border Guard. His face broke into a grin when I joined the queue.

'Izzy.' He seemed absurdly pleased to see me.

'Wilfred.' I returned his smile. It was impossible not to get swept up in his enthusiasm.

'No need to wait,' he said. 'Rako is briefing the second years. You'll be joining them.'

Every head in the line turned to stare at me. No doubt they were all wondering the same thing I was. Why did I get to join the second years?

I slammed my mouth shut and nodded at him. No need for them to know I was as confused as they were.

'Come on Scruffy,' I said, picking up my bag.

Wilfred ruined my cool exit by punching me on the arm. I was sure he meant it in a comradely way, but his fist bit deep into the muscle and I staggered to the side.

The grin on his face intensified to outright merriment. I rubbed my arm, stared him in the eye and said, 'You'll keep.'

He smacked his hands together and said, 'Excellent.'

Rako was standing inside the entry to the building. I paused for a second to admire the old, stone structure with its sweeping pillars and high arches. Colourful banners and wooden plaques lined the walls.

Rako ended my contemplation of the beautiful, old building. 'You're late, and he's not white.'

'I only promised washed-yesterday white,' I said.

'I guess he'll do. First door on the left.' He pointed down a hall. 'Briefing is in five minutes.'

'Ahhh,' I said, 'Wilfred said I'm joining the second years.'

'You don't think you're up to it?' His eyes bored into mine as he frowned.

'I guess the important thing is if *you* think I'm up to it.' While I liked the idea of skipping a year of training, I wasn't sure why they were letting me.

He snorted. 'You're going to have to fight for it, but you're up to it.'

Fight for it? What in the Dark Sky did he mean by that?

I trotted down the hall to the room Rako had indicated. An easy murmur of conversation, punctuated with laughter, flowed out the door to the hallway. Twelve young men sat with their chairs pulled into a rough circle. Some of them were obviously full-blooded faeries; the others must have been the same as me – half-breeds. As soon as I entered the room the conversation stopped, and once again, all eyes were on me.

This time though, the looks were openly hostile. I gulped as I took in their angry looks. *Now* I knew what Rako was talking about. Fight for it indeed.

I was guessing Little Miss Nice wasn't going to cut it with these bad boys. The problem was that I didn't really have any other persona. I scuttled to the back of the room and dived into a chair, opening up the manual that was on the table next to me and burying my head in it.

I could feel their eyes on me, but I stoically ignored them, flicking through the manual whilst not seeing one word. Eventually their conversation started up again and I let out the breath I had been holding.

A few minutes later, total silence fell over the room again and an accented voice asked, 'Who do I have to beat the shit out of to get a seat?'

I knew that voice. My eyes flew to the figure standing in the doorway.

Oh boy, did I *ever* know that voice.

Isgranelda's blonde hair was pulled back into a braid. She wore a skin-tight, black cat suit. I felt like a child as I viewed the ample curves that suit clung to. The zip, running the length of the front, was undone far enough to show her breasts bulging out of her bra. I was thinking she needed a bigger cup size, but I don't think the boys agreed.

'You can sit right here,' one of the bigger men said, patting his lap.

She smiled as she swayed towards him and reached out as if to pat his cheek. Instead, she grabbed his arm and wrenched him out of the chair, pivoting her body to propel him across the room. He flew an impressive distance before crashing face first onto the floor. Then she dusted off her hands and daintily took his seat.

I groaned inwardly. I *so* should have done that. But no, I'd gone for the church-mouse approach and now I would probably *never* earn their respect.

Rako strode through the door. 'Get up Brad,' he said as he stepped over the prone man.

Brad pushed himself onto all fours and then clambered to his feet. I had thought Isgranelda's trick would have made him angry, but instead he eyed her lustily. 'Maybe we can try that again later,' he said, dragging another seat to the front.

'Next time I use my knives.'

I couldn't believe it. What was Isgranelda doing here? The fact that she was part-faery made total sense. Her ability to tie me in knots was her manipulating air.

I stared at the back of her head, wishing her anywhere but there. Perhaps it would be different to school. Perhaps without her friends she wouldn't feel the need to make my life miserable.

Yeah right!

I managed to push thoughts of her aside and concentrate as Rako outlined the program for the year. At the top of the list was the fighting training: swordplay; archery; hand-to-hand combat; and miscellaneous weaponry. Then there was tracking and evasion, first aid, bushcraft and logistics.

'As second years you will become more than proficient in all of these areas, or face dismissal. This year you will also start entering Trillania.'

A few of the students murmured to each other. It seemed I wasn't the only person who didn't know what Trillania was.

'You will be accompanied by Guards for these trips, and it is imperative that you stay with your Guards and obey their every command.'

Trillania? It didn't even ring a faint bell.

'Rosters for training and for Trillania are in the normal place. Take your gear to your barracks and get ready for your first lesson.'

I was more clueless when he strode from the room than I had been when he'd arrived. The only thing to be done was to follow the rest of the class and hope I got some answers as the day went on.

The notice board's normal place was in the entry hall. I stayed at the back of the pack as they clustered in front of it, pushing and shoving to get the best view. Isgranelda elbowed her way into the crowd. From the 'ouches,' and surreptitious rubbing of body parts I gathered she was pinching her way to the front of the group.

'Archery,' she said in her distinctive accent. 'Twenty rumbles I'll wipe the floor with any of you.'

'I'll take you on,' Brad said.

'Anyone else game?' She looked around the group.

'Looks like it's just you and me.' Brad seemed to like that idea.

Once the main group had moved off, I scanned the board. Archery this morning, bushcraft this afternoon, and then, after dinner, Trillania. I had the day to find out what in the Great Dark Sky it was.

The second year barracks was along a corridor and up a flight of winding stairs. A large open room looked out over a field where archery boards stood. One side of the room was lined with bookshelves packed full of books. The rest of the room housed over-stuffed chairs arranged haphazardly around low tables.

A huge chamber opened off the common room. Beds, separated from each other by a wardrobe and a chest of drawers, lined the walls. There didn't seem to be any separate accommodation for Isgranelda and me.

I gathered by the way she dumped her bag on a bed and growled, 'Mine,' that she didn't care. I, however, wasn't sure how I felt about the idea. I chose a bed as far from her as possible and set my bag down on it. Scruffy jumped up, turned around a few times and put his head on his front paws.

'What's with the dog?'

I turned to the young man who had taken the bed next to mine. 'Scruffy is my familiar.'

He stared at Scruffy, a perplexed look puckering his face. Then he flashed me a quick grin. 'Cool.' A little, ginger cat jumped onto his bed and stared across at Scruffy. 'This is Tinker.' It arched its back and padded at the course, grey blanket with its claws before settling down in a position that mimicked Scruffy's.

'I'm Isadora. Izzy for short.' I held my hand out.

He grasped it and pumped it up and down a few times. 'Jared,' he said.

'Hey Jar Head,' one of the other guys yelled out, 'you trying to get the jump on the Ice Queen?'

Ice Queen? Well I guessed that was better than Scaredy Cat.

Jared flipped a finger at the other guy. 'Don't worry about Lance. He's all bark.'

Isgranelda was unpacking her bag onto her bed. Pairs of lacy bras were piled high next to G-string knickers. Brad and a couple of the other guys were watching her with huge grins on their faces. I grimaced and hoped nobody got a look at my very sensible underwear.

'So,' Jared perched on the edge of his bed and nodded his head at Isgranelda, 'what's her story?'

Geez, how to answer that?

'Don't know much about her,' I said. 'She showed up at my school about six months ago and took over as head bully.'

He nodded his head at Brad and said, 'They'll get on well then.'

I opened the top drawer of my dresser and shovelled my underwear in, then put the rest of my clothing into the other ones. I hadn't brought anything that needed hanging. A quick glance at the clock showed that we only had five minutes till we were due at the archery range.

Jared finished putting his clothes into his drawers and then the two of us left the others to their ogling of the contents of Isgranelda's wardrobe. I had no idea how she had managed to wedge so much stuff into one bag.

'Jared,' I didn't want my potentially only friend to think I was an idiot, but I had to ask someone, 'what's Trillania?'

'I'm not sure. I've heard the word before but nobody here ever tells us what it is.'

'Guess we'll find out tonight.'

He nodded his head and led me out a side door and down to the field I had seen from the common room window. Wilfred was already there with a pile of bows and arrows.

'Where are the rest of them?' he asked.

'Unpacking.' I had forgotten how hairy he was. Orange hair covered his arms and sprouted out from under the neck of his shirt.

'You're imagining me naked aren't you?'

I jumped and blushed. I hadn't been imagining it, but I had been wondering if the hair was like that all over his body.

'Hoi Aethan,' he yelled out, 'your woman wants to see me naked.'

There was so much wrong with *that,* that I didn't know where to start refuting information. To start with, I wasn't Aethan's woman. We'd fought together and had one courting session (I wasn't sure what else to call it), but I wasn't his woman and didn't know if I ever would be.

'I do not,' I said, my cheeks on fire.

Aethan laughed as he walked towards us from the targets. He didn't seem disturbed by the mention of me being his woman.

'You and he,' Jared waved a finger between Aethan and me.

'It's complicated,' I said. I didn't want to claim it and yet I found myself strangely reluctant to deny it. The man *was* an eye-fest.

I was thankful when he left it at that and turned his attention to Wilfred. 'Izzy was asking about Trillania.'

Wilfred's bushy eyebrows rose up his forehead, 'But she already…'

'Wilfred.' Aethan's voice was sharp as he shared a 'look' with his friend.

'Oh right,' Wilfred mumbled.

'Don't worry, we'll go through it all this evening before we start,' Aethan said.

I wanted to ask, 'Start what?' but by then he was standing close enough to be a distraction.

It wasn't that his face was perfect in its symmetry but more that the different angles and planes of his cheeks and nose created a face simultaneously rugged and handsome. And then of course there were his eyes, intense in the depth of their colour and unnerving in their intelligence.

Even without the body to match the face I would have found his presence disturbing, so instead of trying to phrase an intelligent sentence I just nodded.

Before I could make an idiot of myself, Isgranelda, followed by the rest of the class, sauntered out onto the field. Her sweeping gaze stopped at Aethan. She licked her lips as she eyed him up and down.

I resisted a groan as I backed away from him, but her eyes flitted to me, took in how close we had been standing and then filled with something – Triumph? Glee? – that had me swallowing nervously.

'You're late,' Aethan barked at them. 'Grab a bow, two to a target.'

Jared picked a bow and I followed him to the furthest target. Should I mention that I had never tried archery?

I watched him place an arrow onto the bowstring. That didn't look so hard. He stood side onto the target, lifted the bow in front of him, pulled back and released the arrow. It flew through the air and I heard a faint thunk as it thudded into the target.

'Bull's eye,' Jared said, handing me the bow.

I picked up an arrow and sat it against the string. Then I started to pull back.

'Stop,' Jared said. 'What are you doing?'

'Shooting?' I pulled a face.

I heard Isgranelda let out a laugh. 'You owe me twenty rumbles.'

Oh great – of course *she* could shoot.

'Best of three.' Brad wasn't taking losing lying down.

'You've never done this before have you?' Jared asked.

I shook my head. 'That obvious?'

'You could say that. Here let me show you.' He placed the end of the arrow over the string. 'This is called nocking the arrow. See how I have the arrow positioned so that the fletching faces away from the string?'

'Ahuh.'

'Now gently wrap the first three fingers of your bowstring hand below the arrow shaft.'

'You need to correct her stance first.'

I jumped at the sound of Aethan's voice and the arrow flew out of my hand and landed point down a few inches from his foot. 'I can't be held responsible for what I do if you're going to sneak up on me,' I muttered as he handed me back the arrow.

They spent the next ten minutes correcting my stance and teaching me how to draw the bow and aim at the target. By the time they said I was ready I was itching to release the arrow.

I sighted up the bowstring, lining the bull's eye up with the centre of the bow limbs, then I took a deep breath and, as I exhaled, I released the arrow. It flew wildly over the top of the target, disappearing into the thicket of trees behind.

'Buzznuckle. What did I do wrong?'

'You pulled back as you released.' It was nice of Jared to sound sympathetic.

I let him fire off a few more arrows before trying again. This time I concentrated on keeping the bow steady, but the arrow embedded itself into the earth a few feet in front of the target. The next arrow flew wide, almost landing on the adjacent target instead.

I listened to Aethan and Wilfred hand out tips to the other second years as I waited for Jared to have his turn.

'Push your fingers out of the way of the bowstring.'

'The release must be executed cleanly in a single smooth action.'

'Rotate your hips so that your lower back is flat.'

There were so many different things to remember that I was getting confused trying to assimilate them. Instead of getting closer to the target, my arrows were getting further away. Some of the others had started placing bets on what I would hit next. I pretended to ignore them but inwardly I cringed at each comment.

Jared was lined up, looking down his arrow at the target when I had the weirdest feeling, as if he were aiming at the wrong thing. As if there were something far more important he should be shooting at. I tried to ignore it but the feeling grew stronger, morphing from urge to impulse.

'Your turn.' Jared handed me the bow and stuck a few arrows head down into the grass within easy reach.

I tried to ignore the feeling now clambering in my head. I *had* to hit that damned target.

'Ten rumbles she misses by more than three feet.'

'That's not a fair bet. That last arrow was wide by more than five.'

'What's she even doing here? She obviously isn't Border Guard material.'

I pushed their voices out of my head, concentrating on the target, seeing only the target, but the feeling persisted, growing in strength and size till it threatened to burst out of me. I hadn't felt it since the last day of school but I recognised it now. It was the raging roar of power soaking through my pores.

'Have… to… hit… the… target.' I clenched my teeth and lifted the bow, releasing a small surge of the energy with the arrow. I had another arrow nocked and released before the first one struck the centre of the target. The second one struck home, splitting my first arrow as I released the third one, but even though I was releasing the energy with the arrows it continued to boil and grow.

I grabbed the last arrow and reached out with my senses.

There. In the trees. Everything in me screamed to aim into those trees.

I jerked the bow sideways away from the target and released my arrow. Shrill laughter followed my wildly divergent shot, but I knew it flew true.

A loud bellow was followed by shaking branches and a goblin staggered out from within the thicket. One hand clutched the arrow protruding from his chest, but the other one held a cross bow. He raised the bow, pointing it towards Aethan.

'Assassin,' Wilfred yelled, pulling his sword from its scabbard. Time seemed to slow as he ran towards the goblin.

A few of the students nocked arrows but I knew they would be too late.

Aethan dived to the side and a bolt twanged and thudded into the ground a few inches from his head.

I raised my arms towards the goblin and released a wave of power. The torrent struck, lifting him bodily into the air. Higher and higher he flew, the crossbow falling from his fingers as he twisted and screamed.

But it wasn't enough, never enough.

I thought of the damage the goblins had done: the people injured; the lives lost. I clenched my fists and twisted my hands and the spinning goblin exploded into a million tiny pieces.

'Now *that's* what I'm talking about!' The rest of the students stared, but Wilfred punched an arm in the air as the gristly parcels rained down on us, covering us all in gore.

Chapter Nine

Dream A Little Dream For Me

The rest of the day turned into a search of the campus for goblins. Only when every square inch of the ground had been searched, and no other goblins found, did Rako allow us to stop.

'Have a shower, get some grub and then meet at the door to the dungeon,' he said. 'Not you.' He pointed a finger at me. 'In my office now.'

I followed him to a room on the second floor. A large table, covered in stacks of files, dominated the room. I took a seat across the table from him.

He leant back in his chair and stared at me from under his bushy eyebrows. 'Would you care to tell me how you knew the goblin was there?'

I squirmed in my seat. 'I just had an urge,' I said. 'A need to shoot into the trees.'

'Dumb blind luck?' he asked.

I shook my head. 'Twice now I've had a pressure build inside me. This time it made me want to do that.'

'What happened the other time?'

'I levitated a room full of students.'

He let out a low whistle. 'That's some kind of fire power you're packing.'

I shifted uncomfortably. 'I can't control it.'

He flicked open a folder and started to make notes. 'Go clean up,' he said.

After I had scrubbed myself and Scruffy, I used the small mirror I'd brought with me for the specific purpose of contacting Mum and Sabby. Grams was with Mum, and after I finally managed to get away, giving them details of my archery lesson but nothing else, I only had a few minutes to make it to the stairs above the dungeon.

I arrived a few seconds before Rako did. He unlocked a large lock and I followed the rest of my class down the dimly lit stairs.

The stairs led to a series of large rooms, each containing a circle of beds. Twelve in total, the beds dominated the centre, arranged like the numbers of a clock; feet to the middle, heads to the edge.

'Right,' Rako said, rubbing his hands together. 'Tonight you're going to learn about a Border Guard's most sacred duty. You've all heard of dream-walkers?' He stopped and looked around the circle. 'So you know that dream-walkers can enter the Land of Dreams in an alert state. They are aware of their surroundings and able to remember their time there when they wake.'

Everybody was nodding at him, urging him to go on.

'We call this land they go to Trillania. What is not common knowledge is that all people go to Trillania when they dream. Dream-walkers roam amongst these dreaming spirits.'

There was a low murmur as Jared put his hand in the air. 'Are the sleeping people aware of the dream-walkers?'

'They can become aware. That is one of the dangers of dream-walking. Frightened dreamers can become violent, and damage sustained in Trillania is sustained on the body in this world.'

That lined up with what Wolfgang had told me. 'You said *one* of the dangers,' I said.

'There are a number of deadly creatures only found there. On top of that, goblins and their minions can also access Trillania.' He began pacing backwards and forwards in front of us. 'Our job as Border Guards is to protect the dreamers, and to do it without them knowing we are there.'

Lance put his hand up and when Rako nodded his head at him said, 'But how are we to protect them without letting them know we are there?'

Rako looked thoughtful for a moment. 'Let me rephrase that. It's not so much that they can't know we are there, but more that they can't realise we're not a part of their dream.'

'So one of our jobs as Border Guards is to protect people while they sleep?' I wanted to make sure I had this correct.

'We guard all of the lands, especially Trillania.'

'Why doesn't anybody know about this?' Isgranelda asked.

'How do you think the average person would cope knowing they are in more danger when they are asleep than awake?'

That was an excellent question. I had always considered going to sleep to be a restful thing. If I had thought for one moment, that the land of dreams was a dark and dangerous place, I would have been too scared to sleep. And a world full of people too scared to sleep would not be a pretty place.

'So,' Brad said, 'we protect the people but we can't let them know that we do it.'

As Brad was speaking Wilfred entered the room carrying a tray covered with small cups. Each cup held a foul-smelling concoction. I wrinkled my nose and pulled away in disgust. Were we expected to drink that?

'It is our secret duty, unknown to any but us, and it must remain this way for all of time.'

Wilfred circulated with the platter, handing a cup to everybody in the class.

'This spell,' Rako held the cup in the air, 'will bind the truth to you. You will be unable to talk of this to any who have not also been bound. But more importantly, you will be unable to speak of this if anyone not bound by this spell is within hearing.'

Well that explained how they managed to keep it secret within their own barracks.

'If you're not willing to drink the spell, all memories of this night will be erased from your mind and you will leave the Border Guards.'

I noticed a few of the boys looking uncertainly at the cup but none refused to drink it when Rako said, 'Bottoms up.'

The spell tasted as bad as it smelt. A putrid concoction of swamp and dead animal that lingered long after the liquid was gone. A chilled tingle swept over my body, buzzing on the surface of my skin.

As Wilfred collected the empty cups, Aethan entered the room with a handful of Border Guards. He was carrying an ornate wooden box, inlaid with metallic patterns. When he lifted the lid, I could see a row of chunky armbands made from leather and the same metal that was inlaid in the box.

He held one in the air. 'We will be using these to transport us to Trillania. These allow us all to become dream-walkers.'

He started to hand out the armbands. 'We will be going in, two Border Guards per student. We will stay in Trillania for ninety minutes before waking.'

There were so many questions I wanted to ask, but I shut my mouth until he handed me an armband.

'Do I need one of these?' I mean according to them I *was* a dream-walker.

'Rako and I have discussed it at great length. We think this will allow all of you to go to Trillania, not just your Fae part.'

I felt a thrum of excitement. Maybe the armband would help join my two parts. Maybe I would remember.

I wasn't sure if I wanted to remember things that might entail my blushing furiously right at that point in time, but beggars can't be choosers so I snapped the armband onto my right arm and closed my eyes.

Nothing happened. No rush of memories. No flash of lightning. Nothing. I opened my eyes to see Aethan grinning at me.

'What did you think was going to happen?' he asked.

Feeling silly, I shrugged my shoulders. 'I'm not sure.'

'Excellent.' Wilfred punched me on the shoulder. 'We're up first.'

'You and me?' I was a little intimidated by the hairy man and the fact that he seemed to know me so well.

'You, me, and my main man.' He nodded his head at Aethan.

I chose a bed, stretching out on it and trying to look relaxed. Scruffy jumped up onto the bed and curled up by my feet, laying his head on my ankle. Wilfred lay down on the bed to my right and Aethan the one on my left. Isgranelda, Brad, and Jared were positioned at the other points of the circle, with a Border Guard on either side of them.

Oh great. My first official trip to Trillania and Isgranelda was coming along for the ride.

I stared at the ceiling, feeling ridiculous, and wide awake. There was no *way* I was going to be able to sleep in this circumstance. Not with a dozen people staring, not with Aethan lying right next to me. But one of the other Border Guards, with sweeping ears that characterised him as a faery, began to hum a low song.

Almost too soft to hear, the melody wrapped around me, relaxing my muscles, turning my limbs to dead weights. One minute I was wide awake, and the next I was standing in Trillania.

***

Wilfred let out a roar and rushed towards me, sweeping me up in his arms and swinging me around.

'What the…?' I squealed, pushing him away from me as soon as my feet were on the ground.

He peered at me, a disappointed look on his face. 'You don't remember?'

'I wish I did.'

He shook his head and stomped off, muttering under his breath.

'All right everybody, gather round,' Aethan said. 'Ninety minutes, that's all. Teach them the basics, keep them safe.'

The other Border Guards nodded their heads before reaching out and linking hands with their student. In the blink of an eye they were gone.

'Where did they go?'

'Wherever they wanted to,' Wilfred said. 'That's the beauty of Trillania. Here you can move with the merest of thoughts.' There was a sulky edge to his voice.

'That's also why you have to be careful what you think about,' Aethan said.

'Right,' I said, 'so lesson number one, be careful what you think.'

'That sums up lessons one, two and three,' Wilfred said.

'Where are we going?' I asked.

'Let's check out what's happening in London,' Aethan said.

I reached out and grasped his and Wilfred's hands. The world blurred around us and suddenly we were standing in Trafalgar Square.

Music resonated and light shone at the far end of the Square. 'What's going on?' I asked, peering toward the light.

'Looks like a dance,' Wilfred said. 'Excellent. How do I look?' He ran his hands over his hair and beard, rearranging the tousled locks into place.

'Like a huge, red bear,' I said.

'Just the look I was going for.' He marched off towards the party.

'They can see us,' Aethan said, 'but we mustn't take the focus away from their dream. Ugly things can happen if you do.' He also started walking towards the dancers.

That was it? That was the brief? Ugly things can happen?

I shook my head and followed after him and Wilfred. What sort of ugly things?

Aethan and Wilfred stopped in the shadow of a doorway near where the dancers twirled. Women, dressed in flowing gowns, floated effortlessly in the arms of the men who led them. Jewels glittered on arms and necks, and hair tumbled from elaborate styles. The men were no less glamorous than the women, wearing heavily-brocaded vests on fine-silk shirts, studded with diamond and ruby buttons.

'They're all here together?'

'It's not uncommon for dreamers of like-minded pursuits to find each other.'

The dancers wove an intricate pattern with their feet and their bodies; swirling and turning, leaping and whirling, never once running into another dancer.

I was tapping a foot in time with the music, enjoying the entertainment when I felt it - the strange surge inside me. The same feeling I'd had that morning.

'Let's go see what else is happening in London.' Aethan started to turn away from the dancers.

'Wait.' I grabbed his hand. 'Something is wrong.' The feeling grew. I stared at the dancers, trying to pinpoint its cause.

'What is it?' Wilfred and Aethan stared at the dancers as well.

'I'm not sure,' I said. 'I think it's one of the dancers.'

Wilfred and Aethan exchanged a look. 'We're going to have to go in for a closer look,' Wilfred said, 'and I can't dance.'

'We can't go in there like this.' I gestured at my jeans and shirt.

'You know how we said we can change Trillania with a thought?' Aethan's clothes changed from leather and fur to a navy-blue brocade vest over a white silk shirt. Black pants completed the outfit.

I closed my eyes and visualised one of the dresses I had been admiring on a ravishing redhead. Wilfred let out a low wolf-whistle and when I opened my eyes I was wearing an exact replica of the dress. The neckline plunged far deeper than I had expected.

'Very good,' Aethan said. I wasn't sure if he was referring to my changing my clothes or to my choice of clothes. He held a hand out to me, and, when I placed my hand upon it, swept me into his arms and onto the floor.

Cocooned in his arms I felt like a precious object as he spun me and dipped me, and for one brief moment I forgot our reason for being there. For that second I was just a woman and he just a man, enjoying the feel of our bodies moving together and of skin touching skin.

The power surged inside me, pulling my attention back to the present. Someone was here with evil intent, and I had to find them.

Aethan wove us skilfully through the dance floor and we quickly made a complete circuit, coming back to the edge near Wilfred.

'See anything?' he asked.

I was about to say no, but suddenly, just like that morning, I could pinpoint where the pressure wanted me to go.

'That way.' I nodded my head to where the feeling was strongest, and started to drag Aethan towards it. We immediately collided with an older man escorting a pretty, young, blonde woman.

'What do you think you're doing?' The man asked, his face screwed up in anger.

As soon as they stopped dancing, another couple collided with them. It only took a moment for the previously well-ordered dance floor to become chaotic. Angry voices could be heard from all areas and previously happy dreamers turned to stare at Aethan and me.

At the far side of the gathering a tall man stood by himself. He met my eyes and his face took on a mocking look as he shimmered and changed. The svelte, blonde man was replaced by a goblin. He lifted a hand in farewell and faded from view.

Wilfred pulled my attention back to the dreamers. 'Uh oh,' he said. 'Do something before…'

'Things get ugly,' I said, as the man in front of me brandished a knife.

'Kiss her,' Wilfred hissed.

'What?' Who did he want me to kiss? The blonde?

The crowd surged towards us, furious at our interference. Things were definitely getting ugly.

'For Sky's sake Aethan, *kiss her.*'

I turned to look at Wilfred, but Aethan clasped my face with his hands and lowered his mouth to mine. For a second I struggled against him. I mean what was he thinking? We were about to get attacked. But that concern only lasted for a second. Then I totally forgot about the crowd.

I forgot about the goblin.

I forgot where we were.

I forgot what we were meant to be doing.

The feel of him, the smell of him, consumed me.

One of his hands left my face, snaking around my waist and pulling me in tight. The pressure on my mouth became harder, more urgent, and I returned it with pleasure. It wasn't nearly enough. Feelings I had never experienced before zinged through my body. I wanted more of him, needed more of him; needed to feel his skin, needed to feel his body. I wanted to roll in him, drown in him, swallow him whole.

It took a while for Wilfred's voice to penetrate the fog of my mind.

'Guys,' he hissed. 'You can stop now.'

Stop? I didn't want to stop. I'd only just started.

Aethan released his hold on me and stepped back. Panting slightly he stared into my eyes. 'That was… interesting,' he murmured.

Interesting? Amazing, awesome, breathtaking - *those* were the words that sprung to my mind when I thought about that kiss, not interesting.

I took a deep breath and tore my gaze from his. The dreamers had returned to their dancing. 'What happened?'

'By being more interested in each other we were no longer directly influencing their dream.'

I could feel a wide grin split my face. 'So do you two,' I pointed my finger between them, 'use that ploy often?'

'Ha ha,' Wilfred said, ruffling up my hair the most annoying way possible. 'You going to wear that dress all night?'

With a start I realised Aethan had returned to his former clothing. I felt a blush start on my cheeks as I followed his example.

'Can you still feel it?' Aethan asked.

He really wasn't helping with my blushing problem. *Of course* I could still feel it. That kiss wasn't something I was going to stop feeling for a very long time.

'Which way did it go?' Wilfred asked.

And that was when I realised they were asking about my previous feeling, *not* the kiss.

'Oh right.' Just call me volcano-face and be done with it. 'I haven't felt it since… I mean I couldn't feel it once…' Wilfred chuckled and I sighed and mumbled, 'He's gone.'

Aethan nodded his head and then said, 'I'd like to show you our homeland.'

He took one of my hands while Wilfred took the other, the world shimmered again and this time I was staring at a wooded wonderland.

Everywhere I looked, little lights floated through the trees, giving off a soft, luminous glow. Aethan held his hand out and a light drifted over to him and rested on one of his fingers.

'What is it?' I asked, moving in to get a closer look.

'It's a faery.'

'But it's so small.'

'There are many different varieties of faeries. This is a garden faery. We are land faeries.'

'Is it really here?'

'It is dreaming.' He lifted his hand higher and the faery floated off, continuing its leisurely dance through the trees.

We followed after it, winding our way down through the forest.

'What other sorts of faeries are there?' There was so much I didn't know.

'Sprites,' Aethan replied.

Wilfred let out a snort. 'Don't let one of *them* get close. They bite.'

Aethan nodded his head. 'Sprites are mischievous. In contrast, pixies are friendly. And of course we can't forget the night faeries.'

'I've never heard of night faeries,' I said.

'They are the dark side of our light, the night to our day.'

The trees thinned around us and we stepped out onto a field. In the distance, a building soared above us. Not that the word 'building' really did it justice. It reminded me of a whimsically-iced cake; turrets and stone lacework hanging from every possible position. The windows were filled with light, and music tinkled towards us on the breeze.

'It's beautiful.'

'Isilvitania Castle,' Aethan said. 'Although you know it as Eynsford Castle.'

'Eynsford Castle?' Eynsford Castle was a dilapidated ruin in the centre of the village. 'But how can that be?'

'Our land is a copy of your land.'

'I don't understand,' I said.

'Hmmm, how best to explain it?' He paused for a minute while he thought. 'Imagine laying a piece of tracing paper over a map and copying that image onto the paper. Our land is like that. It is there, but totally separate at the same time.'

I tried to get my head around it. 'So, it's like your land is floating above ours?' I finally said.

'Not floating. They co-exist, parted by the veils.'

'So then Trillania?'

'Trillania is like a traced copy of both of those lands, but everyplace is everywhere, accessible by mere thought.'

Now I was really confused. 'But…'

The power pulsed through me again, pulling me towards the castle. 'Come on,' I yelled, running towards it.

Aethan grabbed my hand and suddenly we were at the entrance. I raced through the door and up a flight of stairs, climbing until I could go no further. I turned left and ran down the hallway and suddenly, I could hear fighting.

'The Royal Apartments,' Aethan said, racing past me. He threw the door open to reveal half a dozen goblins fighting two Border Guards and a faery wearing pyjamas.

'Father,' Aethan cried, pulling a sword out of the air. He slashed at the head of one of the goblins attacking King Arwyn. Headless, the goblin fell to the ground and then shimmered from view.

Wilfred engaged another goblin and there was no room for me to join the fight. If I tried, I was as likely to hurt an ally as an enemy. But that didn't stop the pressure from growing, from demanding that I do something, anything but stand there and watch.

My skin felt stretched tight, breathing was difficult, stars started to twirl in front of my eyes as I struggled to hold onto the power. In pure desperation, terrified of what might happen - it felt entirely possible that this time ***I*** might be the one to explode - I threw my arms out to the sides.

Stone roared as it exploded outwards, leaving two massive holes where the side walls of the room had been. The fighters seemed oblivious to the damage as chunks of ceiling fell into the holes.

Uh Oh.

'Ah Aethan.' How best to get his attention without getting him killed? I waited while he ducked a sword swing and thrust upwards with his. He skewered the goblin through the chest and then kicked it off his blade.

'Aethan.' I raised my voice as the ceiling started to creak.

He spun towards me and I grimaced and pointed at the holes.

He gaped at the wreckage and then looked up at the ceiling. It was rippling slowly. 'We have to get out of here,' he yelled. He lunged for his father, grabbing onto him with a hand and fading from view. The two other Guards flickered out of sight straight after them. The four goblins still standing turned their attention to Wilfred and me.

'Time to go.' Wilfred reached out and took my hand.

I heard a roar as the ceiling started to cave in, and then we were standing in Trillania where we had crossed over. The next second I was staring at the ceiling in the sleep room. Scruffy was still guarding my bed and Brad, Jared, and Isgranelda had already been replaced by other students.

'I'm assuming that wasn't a pleasure jaunt,' Rako said, looking at his watch. We had missed our ninety minute curfew.

'Goblins attacked the Faery Royal suite.' Aethan climbed off his bed.

'They are safe?'

'Only father was there.'

Rako shook his head. 'More and more the attacks seem to be centred on Isilvitania. What is she up to?'

'What is who up to?' I whispered to Wilfred.

'Galanta, their Queen.'

'I want to be fully briefed on this later.' Rako clapped his hands together. 'All right you lot. Everybody take a dream-catcher and go get some sleep.'

'Ah Wilfred,' I said, 'did I just blow holes in the real castle?'

He laughed and shook his head. 'What's in Trillania is a representation of the real world, not the other way around.' He handed me a shield made of the same materials as the dream-walker armbands.

'What's this?'

'Hang it on your bed. It will stop you entering Trillania when you sleep. Especially important for you. We don't want you dream-walking unsupervised.'

I weighed it in my hand. 'Why don't we give these to the public? Or at least important targets?'

'They only work if you have used one of the armbands.'

I was too wound up to sleep when I got back to the room, and, if I were entirely truthful, a little worried about sleeping in a room full of people. I hung the dream-catcher on the end of my bed and took Scruffy's brush out. Much to his disgust, I gave him a thorough grooming. He looked just as bad when I finished as he had when I had begun, but the calming sensation of running the brush through his hair had soothed my frantic mind.

I turned off my little light, tucked Scruffy into my side, and closed my eyes. Much to my surprise I was soon fast asleep, not waking until the morning.

Chapter Ten

Isadora And The Three Buffos

'Hey sleepy head.' The voice and a hand on my shoulder woke me. Jared stood looking down at me, an amused expression on his face. His lips were bright red. 'You really need to look in a mirror.'

I needed to look in a mirror? The man was wearing make-up.

I clawed my way up out of bed and searched through my top drawer till I found my communication mirror. Somebody, and I had my suspicions on whom that somebody might be, had drawn a moustache on my face. It was long and black and curled at the edges.

'How,' I asked, 'am I going to get this off my face?'

'You can't.' He pointed at his lips.

I stifled a giggle. 'I thought you were wearing lipstick.'

'I wish.'

I looked at Scruffy. 'Call yourself a guard dog?' He stretched out fully into my half of the bed, totally unconcerned by our new facial features.

I pulled open my drawers and took out a shirt.

Jared put a hand on my arm. 'Uniform from today,' he said. 'You'll find it hanging in your wardrobe.'

I opened my wardrobe to find a variety of clothing hanging there: black tank tops, t-shirts and leather pants; and black boots that laced to the knee. Two pairs of charcoal and black camouflage-print pants, a couple of fur vests and a black, long-sleeved shirt made from the softest leather, completed my uniform. I grabbed a black tank top and a pair of the camouflage pants.

'Wait for me,' I said, heading for the bathroom. 'I'll only be a few minutes.' There was no way I was going to breakfast by myself with this thing on my face.

I threw some water over my cheeks, scrubbing at my moustache for a few seconds before ascertaining that Jared was correct – it wasn't coming off the easy way.

Giving up, I pulled my hair back into a long braid and climbed into my uniform. I often had trouble finding pants long enough for me, so I was pleased to find that the clothing fit perfectly. I pulled on the boots and laced them up hastily.

Jared was sitting on the edge of his bed waiting for me. Scruffy was on one side of him and Tinka on the other. Both his hands were busy scratching behind their ears.

'How do I look?' I pointed at my face.

'Ridiculous, but you'll do.'

There was the expected amount of sniggering when we entered the mess for breakfast. I kept my eyes to the front and tried to ignore it. Isgranelda and Brad were sitting at a bench together, broad grins on their faces. Jared and I helped ourselves to food and sat at the far end of the hall from them.

I wanted to talk about Trillania, but some of the first years were sitting at the end of our table within hearing. So instead, I concentrated on my food.

'Isadora Scrumpleton?' I looked up from my porridge to find a Border Guard I hadn't met before standing in front of me. 'Rako would like to see you in his office when you are finished breakfast.'

I pulled a face at Jared and stood up. 'Better get it over and done with.'

Rako was sitting at his desk, studying a pile of paperwork. He looked up when I knocked on the open door, seeming pleased to have an excuse to put his paperwork aside

'Have a seat.' He gestured at the stool on the opposite side of his desk and then looked at me with a puzzled expression on his face, but he didn't mention my moustache. 'Just trying to finish your paperwork,' he said, pointing at the pile he had been perusing when I entered.

'That's *my* paperwork?'

'We've been collating information on you for years. True dream-walkers are very rare. Especially ones as powerful as you seem to be.'

I had already guessed from Aethan and Wilfred, and also from what I had seen in my mind, that I had been active in Trillania for years. What I hadn't guessed was that the Border Guards had been collating information on me that whole time.

'I'm not a very good dream-walker,' I said. 'I mean the only time I can remember being in Trillania is last night.'

'I spoke to Wolfgang after his session with you. He has no doubt that once your witch and faery sides become cohesive you will remember.'

I looked at the pile of papers. 'What more do you need from me?'

'Actually it's something quite simple. I just need your next-of-kin details and a photo if you have one.'

I dug around in my pocket for my wallet. I had a photo in there of Mum and Grams that would do. It was an exact replica of one I had in a frame beside my bed. I gave Rako the photo, and Mum and Grams' details.

He placed a blank piece of paper on the table next to the photo and then ran his wand over the photo. An exact replica of it appeared on the sheet of paper.

'Neat,' I said.

'A talent peculiar to my family.' He handed me back the photo. I noticed a mouse peeping out of the top of his shirt pocket as he sat back in his chair and put his arms behind his head. 'Aethan and Wilfred told me what you did last night. The talents you are showing will be immensely useful. They will also mean that you, and whoever you are with, are more likely to be engaged by the enemy. This puts you in more danger than any other student. As such, I expect you to train harder than any other student.'

I managed to suppress a surge of panic. That was exactly what I was here for, to fight, to protect. And if I were able to do that more effectively than any other, then so be it if that put me in danger. What was the alternative? To walk away knowing that I could help? That was no longer an option.

The day flew by (fencing in the morning, woodcraft in the afternoon) and before I knew it, I was strapping on the armband and climbing back onto the bed.

'Wilfred,' Aethan said, 'take Izzy in and wait for me. I'll be a few minutes behind.'

Wilfred nodded and climbed onto the bed next to me. Just as it had last night, the melody of the sleep spell touched me, and within moments I was in Trillania.

'I like what you've done with your hair.' Wilfred smirked as he touched a finger to his own moustache.

I concentrated for a second and could tell by the way his smirk faded that I had managed to remove the stupid thing from my face. No need to wear it here. Then I stared at him, visualising what I wanted, and clapped my hands in delight as all of his facial hair disappeared.

'Hey,' he said. His eyes narrowed and suddenly I was twice my normal width. My clothes strained with the effort of holding in the rolls of fat.

'That's not nice.' I flipped him off and then turned his hands into feet so he couldn't do the same to me.

He hooked an arm around me and rubbed one of his new feet into my face. 'Tell me the truth, do my feet stink?'

His toe hair went up my nose and I squealed and turned his body into that of an orangutan. I backed away from him, laughing at the puzzled expression on his face. He looked down at his shaggy arms and furry belly and said, 'I told you she wanted to see me naked.'

Aethan's laugh alerted me to his presence. I turned myself back to my normal body size (no need for him to see me looking like Ten-Tonne Tessie) and then turned to face him. 'What are we doing tonight?'

'How do you feel about a bit of hunting?' A sword appeared at his waist and a bow and quiver full of arrows over his shoulder. He waved his hand and a black stallion appeared. It stamped its feet and snorted mist into the night.

I squeezed my eyes shut and pictured a white horse with a mane and tail that touched the ground. Her hooves were a dazzling gold and her eyes the brightest blue. I felt warm breath on my face and then her soft lips nibbled my cheek.

Wilfred waved his arm and a bronze horse with a dragon's head appeared. It arched its neck and blew fire into the air. 'Now that's what I'm talking about,' he said as he clambered onto its back.

'Show off,' I said, mentally adding a saddle to my horse. I climbed onto her back and then turned her around to face Aethan. 'Why do we need mounts?'

'We don't. It's just fun.' A boyish grin appeared on his face and then he turned his stallion and raced away into the night.

Wilfred and I leapt after him, my mare running neck-to-neck with his mount.

'Do you like my draghorse?' he asked.

'Did it take you long to think of that?'

'Nah. I'm naturally brilliant.'

I laughed at the feel of the wind in my face and kicked my heels into my horse's sides. She neighed in response and lengthened her pace until it felt like we were flying through the night.

Finally Aethan slowed his pace to a walk and Wilfred and I fell in beside him. 'Nightmare Forest.' Aethan nodded at the tall trees ahead of us. 'Most of the monsters that stalk dreamers are bred in there.'

There was wild laughter and an old man, naked as the day he was born, sprinted from the closest bushes. Still cackling, he disappeared into the distance.

'We go on foot from here.' Aethan's mount disappeared from between his legs and he dropped lightly to the ground.

I tried to emulate his move but ended up on my arse on the soft turf. I ignored Wilfred's outstretched hand and jumped to my feet, dusting myself off.

'It's all in the timing,' Aethan said. It wasn't as large as Wilfred's, but a smile still tugged at the corners of his mouth.

'So what exactly do Border Guard's do in Trillania?' I was still trying to get my head around it.

'There's a rotational roster. We take turns guarding heads of state and any other important political figures.' Aethan headed towards the forest as he spoke.

I started to follow him and tripped over Wilfred's outstretched foot. It was something I would have seen if he hadn't elongated his leg to twice its normal length to do it. 'Game on,' I hissed, dusting myself off again.

'Then there are the roamers.'

'Let me guess,' I said. 'They roam?'

He chuckled. 'Something like that.'

'Har har. They scour the land for evil.' Wilfred was wearing a pirate's hat and eye patch. He slashed at the trees with a cutlass.

'Then there are the hunters.'

'Us? Right?'

Aethan gave me a broad grin. 'Yep, tonight we are hunters.' He pulled an arrow out of his quiver and put it into his bow.

I snaked my arms towards Wilfred, elongating them longer and longer until they were behind him. Then I punched him in the back of his knees, causing his legs to collapse. He fell forwards, landing face first onto the branch-covered ground.

'Agghhh,' he screamed, agony ripping through his voice. He pushed himself back to his knees and a stick protruded from his empty eye socket. Blood dribbled down his face and his eyeball dangled from a white worm-like structure.

'Oh Great Dark Sky,' I shrieked. 'Oh no. I'm so sorry. I didn't mean it.'

Wilfred burst out laughing and the grizzly spectacle disappeared. 'Got ya,' he said, climbing to his feet. He whistled as he walked off.

It took a while for my heartbeat to return to normal and my hands to stop shaking. Then I also placed an arrow on the string of my bow.

The first monster broke from its cover with no warning. Bright-red eyes glowed in its pig-like face, and tusks stabbed from the corners of its mouth, its forehead, and behind its ears.

It stopped when it saw us and shook its head. Saliva flicked out in an arc, flying into the foliage. I heard sizzling and then leaves and branches dropped to the forest floor.

I changed my outfit to a fine layer of tiny metal discs that covered me from the neck down. I didn't know what it was, but I wasn't taking any chances with that thing's drool.

It lowered its head and pawed at the ground with two of its eight legs.

'Spread out.' Aethan moved to the left.

I let Wilfred have the middle as I darted to the right. 'Why aren't we shooting?' I asked as it glared at us with those freaky eyes.

'We don't want to piss off its Mumma,' Wilfred said.

'Mumma?'

Mumma let out a shriek of rage and charged from the trees. I had thought bubba monster was scary, but in comparison to its mother, it was a giggling bundle of joy. Mumma was huge. She towered above us, breathing fire out through the nostrils of her snout. Each of her tusks was a couple of feet long and appeared to be covered in dried blood. Her legs ended in talons, tipped with cruel claws, and when she roared I could see row-after-row of razor-sharp teeth.

'Oh boy,' I said, raising my bow.

'Don't shoot,' Aethan said at the same time that Wilfred said, 'Hold.'

'Let me guess.' I was ashamed to note a tremble in my voice. 'We don't want to piss off Dadda?'

'Give the girl a cigar.'

'Seriously,' I said in horror, 'there's a Dadda?'

Trees shook and trembled and I heard a large branch crash to the ground.

'Oh whizbang,' I said as Dadda squeezed out from between two large oaks.

He stopped and observed his surroundings, intelligence burning bright in his fiery eyes. He stared at the three of us and snorted a trail of fire out of his nostrils. Bubba monster scuttled over to stand under the protection of its father's body, peering out from behind one of the legs.

'This,' Aethan said in a low voice as he backed away from the trio, 'is a family of fire-breathing buffos. Buffos cause a lot of casualties in Trillania. But there are three very good reasons why we don't try to hunt fire-breathing buffos.'

'And those reasons are?' I backed as carefully as I could over the rough terrain.

Dadda pawed at the ground and shook his head, throwing those tusks from side-to-side in a figure of eight pattern.

'They are immune to magic, and their hides are impervious to arrows.'

'That's two,' I said. 'What's the third reason?' I had a really bad feeling about reason number three.

Wilfred slipped his arrow back in his quiver and slung the bow over his back. 'The third reason,' he said, drawing his sword from its sheath, 'is very simple. We don't hunt fire-breathing buffos, because *they* hunt *us*.'

As if it had been waiting for those words, the father buffo broke from its standing position into a sprint. Fire sprayed from its nostrils as it rocketed towards us.

'Over here you ugly bastard,' Wilfred yelled. The buffo altered its course so that it was heading straight for him. Wilfred dropped to the ground and I shrieked as the buffo ran at him. Those talons would tear him to shreds. But Wilfred rolled to the side at the last second, narrowly missing those churning feet. He ripped the tip of his sword down the buffo's belly, opening up a long wound.

The buffo bellowed in rage and turned faster than I would have thought possible, pawing at the ground where Wilfred had been. But the big man moved faster, leaping to his feet and out of the way of those tusks. It charged after him, throwing its head around and spraying an acid rain of saliva. A couple of drops landed on my armour, etching into the metal.

Aethan ran behind the buffo, slashing at its rear with his sword. His strike bounced off its hide. It flicked its tail - a hard, toughened blade - but otherwise paid Aethan no attention. Wilfred ran off, waving his arms and shrieking like a girl.

I let out a wild laugh and charged the buffo from the other side. Using my sword like a lance, I aimed below its ribcage and thrust as hard as I could. Once the tip had penetrated the hide, the rest of the blade slid in easily.

The buffo spun, ripping the handle out of my grasp as it trained its sight on me. Now it was my turn to run. Although *I* didn't have to try to shriek like a girl, it happened quite naturally.

Mumma buffo roared her displeasure and charged, racing straight at Aethan. He dived over her, jumping to his feet and spinning to meet her next charge.

I raced away from him, leading the father in the opposite direction as I ran wildly through the trees. I dodged its flaming breath as I tried to stay ahead.

'Blow it up,' Wilfred yelled.

I leapt from one tree to the next, scrambling higher and higher till I balanced on a thick branch. 'It doesn't work like that,' I said from between clenched teeth.

The Buffo swung its head from side-to-side as it searched the undergrowth for me. It stopped and sniffed the air.

'Well how does it work?' Wilfred's voice was getting closer, but he wouldn't get there before the buffo found me.

'I don't know.' I willed a spear into my hands, sent a prayer up to the Great Dark Sky and then, spear point down, I leapt from my branch onto the back of the buffo. I felt the spear tear its way through hide and muscle and then the buffo took off with me hanging wildly to the spear.

'Get out of the way,' I yelled at Wilfred. I had time to see the astonished look on his face as the buffo ran past. It barged into trees trying to wipe me from its back. I pulled my legs up, relying on the spear embedded through its body to hold me upright.

As the buffo ran through the clearing I braced my legs up under me and jumped off its back, turning a somersault and landing on my feet.

Wilfred charged past me, chasing after Dadda. Aethan was leading Mumma in a merry dance. He held up a shield to protect himself from her fire, and dodged her tusks while he stabbed at her side. Her hide was covered with multiple puncture wounds and blood dribbled onto the ground, but she showed no signs of slowing.

I could try to help him, but I might get in his way and he seemed to be managing her quite well by himself. I was about to follow Wilfred when I felt heat radiating through the metal encasing my back.

I spun around, a blade already in my hand, and there was Baby buffo. I stared into its eyes and felt wretched. It was only a baby, and we were doing our darndest to destroy its family. I felt its grief, I felt its sorrow, and then, as it swung its head at me, I felt its anger.

The tip of its tusk screeched along my armour, catching the edge of the discs at my shoulder and tossing me through the air. I slammed into a tree and slid to the ground. Pain flashed in my head as it connected with a rock.

I crawled to the other side of the tree and huddled there while fire wrapped around the edges. The trees spun in front of me and my head throbbed. Blood dribbled down my forehead into my eye and I brushed it away with the back of my arm.

I staggered through the undergrowth, looking for a hiding spot. It snuffled where I had crouched behind the tree and then let out a satisfied snort. I was guessing it had found my scent. I pulled myself up and leant back against a trunk, shield in one hand and sword in the other. I was hoping the sight of my being armed might slow it and give me time to recover.

No such luck. It pawed the ground and shook its head, spraying droplets of saliva over me. A few landed on my face, burning deep into my skin. And then it charged.

I held up the shield, closed my eyes, and waited for death to find me. But instead of tearing into my flesh the buffo let out a woompha of air. The sound of its hooves beating on the earth changed from rhythmical to comical. I opened my eyes to see it skid along the ground, a score of arrows protruding from its body.

'Izzy got handed her arse by Baby Buffo.' Wilfred had a burn down one side of his face.

'You said its hide was impenetrable to arrows.'

'A full grown adult's is,' Aethan said, hanging his bow back over his shoulder. 'But a baby buffo's hide is as soft as…'

'Baby skin?' I supplied. I pushed myself away from the tree and immediately fell to my knees.

'You're hurt.' Aethan crouched beside me and pushed me down onto the ground.

'I'm fine,' I mumbled. The feel of his hands examining my face was far too nice. 'I hit my head.'

'I think we've had enough hunting for one night.' Aethan helped me up and slung an arm around my back and under my armpit.

'Could I have changed the buffo?' I asked.

'You mean like you and Wilfred were doing to each other?'

'Yes.' I felt stupid for not thinking of it before.

'You can only do that to things that don't exist here in reality.'

'Oh. So other dreamers.'

'Other dreamers.'

Wilfred propped up my other side.

'Time to wake up,' Aethan said, and then I did.

Chapter Eleven

Fool Me Once

I opened my eyes. My head still spun and my face burned where the buffo had sprayed me with its saliva. Scruffy whined and pawed at my leg, and I reached out a hand to him. 'Why do I still hurt?'

'When an injury occurs during dream-walking, the physical manifestations can appear on the body of the walker.'

'Oh.' Someone had told me that before, but my head was too fuzzy to remember whom. 'Why only *can?'*

'Because you bring the injuries back with you when you come.'

'Oh, so if Baby Buffo had succeeded…?'

'You wouldn't have come back at all.'

'You fought buffos?' Rako's voice held tight anger. 'What part of 'keep them safe' did you not understand?'

'We're in trouble,' Wilfred muttered in a sing-song voice.

I looked over at him. The side of his face was a mess. 'That must hurt.'

'Daddio gave almost as good as he got.' His face broke into a grin. 'I almost wet myself when you jumped on his back.'

I started to laugh but it made my head throb. Instead I shut my eyes and said, 'I almost wet *myself* when you ran off shrieking like a girl.'

'I did not shriek like a girl.'

I opened my eyes and peered at him. 'You did too.'

'It would not be possible for me to shriek like a girl. My voice doesn't go that high.'

Headache or not I started to laugh. 'It was funny when I thought you were doing it on purpose. Now it's hysterical.'

I could hear Rako berating Aethan. 'She jumped on his back? Where the hell were you?'

'I was kind of busy at the time. Uh Sir, do you think I can go for the healer?'

Sir? We *must* have been in trouble. I'd never heard Aethan call Rako 'Sir' before.

'I have a mind to let them heal naturally. Would teach you all a lesson.' Rako let out a big huff of air. 'Oh fine, go get Brinda.'

A few minutes later I felt a soft hand on my brow. A tingle passed through me and when I opened my eyes a faery woman stared into my face. 'A head injury and buffo burns,' she said. 'Nothing serious. You've had a busy night young lady.' She laid a hand on either side of my head and I felt a trickle of power seep into me. It reached out like cold fingers into my head and neck. 'Hold steady,' she said.

One second the cold soothed my wounds and the next it heated to a temperature approaching boiling. I screeched and clawed at her hands. Strong arms grabbed mine, forcing them to my side.

'Stay still.' Her voice was firm and merciless as the heat scorched, burning its way out of my body.

I let out a scream and kicked my legs against the bed.

Was she trying to kill me?

As quickly as the heat had come, it flashed and disappeared. Panting, I sagged back against the bed.

She removed her hands from my head. 'It is done. You will need to get plenty of rest and food over the next few days to replenish the energy I just used.'

I felt her weight shift off my bed and then Wilfred said, 'Oh boy, here we go.'

When the memory of the pain had faded I opened my eyes. Aethan sat beside me, still pinning my arms to the bed. Concern filled his eyes. 'I'm sorry. I should never have taken you into the forest.'

I struggled to sit up and he let me go, pulling me up beside him. 'We've hunted before,' I said.

'You remember?' His voice held a measure of relief.

I shook my head. 'During my session with Wolfgang I saw a memory. You admitted you had taught me to hunt.'

Disappointment bloomed in his eyes and he was silent for a moment. 'Once you realised the monsters were there you started hunting them yourself. I couldn't stop you, so I taught you.'

I stared into his beautiful, dark-blue eyes. 'This is no different.'

He met my gaze for a few seconds longer and then nodded. 'I will not stop you. But I *will* keep you safe.'

'We will keep each other safe.'

A grin appeared on his face. 'You are the most stubborn person I know.'

Stubborn? Was that good? I would have preferred mesmerising.

Wilfred let out a bellow and we both rushed to his side. It was over before we got there, the skin on his face as perfect and hairy as it had been.

Rako stalked back into the room. 'Isadora, I want you home for the next few days.'

'But I'm fine.' I really did feel as good as I had before my injury.

'Are you questioning my command?' His voice held a dangerous edge.

'No Sir.' Probably best not to push him any further than we had.

'Correct answer. You will rest and return for duties next week.'

I sighed and pushed away from the beds. What was I going to do for the next five days? After only two days here my old life seemed dull in comparison.

'What shall I tell my family?'

He rubbed the tips of the fingers on one hand up and down the scar on his face and I wondered, not for the first time, how he had got it. 'I will make sure you have enough homework to keep you busy. There will be no need for tricky questions.'

I pulled a face and stomped from the room, making sure that I didn't stomp *so* hard that I drew Rako's attention. I was annoyed, *not* suicidal.

When I got back to the second-year rooms, Jared was sitting cross-legged on his bed with Tinka on his lap. 'What happened?'

'We ran across a family of buffos.'

'Buffos?'

'Huge, angry, fire-breathing pigs.'

'You get all the fun.'

I jumped onto my bed and pulled Scruffy up beside me. He snuggled in close to my leg and stared up at me with his huge, brown eyes.

'He was crying.' Jared nodded his head at Scruffy. 'Like he knew something was wrong.'

I scratched my familiar behind his ears and he lay his head on my knee. 'What did you get up to?'

'Same as last night. We roamed.'

'Anything interesting?'

'Saw a group of people playing naked limbo.' He smiled at the memory. 'Brent said tomorrow night we're hunting.'

'Watch out for the buffos.' I unlaced my boots and bent over to pull one off. My head spun and I grabbed the edge of my bed. 'Whoa.'

Jared grabbed my shoulders and helped me back up. The spinning continued as I lay down.

'Here.' He pulled my boots off and helped me wiggle under the edge of my covers.

'I have to go home tomorrow,' I said. 'Brinda said it would take a few days to get over the healing.'

'I think she might be onto something. You've gone as white as a really, really white thing.'

I let out a low laugh. 'Don't wake me in the morning. Not even if they've given me a matching beard.'

'What about if they've shaved off your eyebrows?'

I smiled. 'Especially not then.'

***

The room was empty and the sun high when I finally woke. Scruffy was curled into my back. I sat up slowly, trying not to disturb him, and grabbed my mirror. Eyebrows still intact and no matching beard. It had been a good night.

A pile of papers lay on my bedside table. The top sheet was a list of recommended reading with a note that the mentioned text books had already been placed in my car. The next few pages contained the assignments that needed to be completed by the end of the term.

I scanned the page: first-aid techniques; methods of lighting fires; how to track at night; wild animals found in Trillania; escape and evasion techniques; and cultural differences between goblins, orcs and trolls.

The last page was written in an elegant script. My breath caught as I realised it was a letter from Aethan requesting the pleasure of my company on Saturday. A knot formed in my stomach at the thought.

It wasn't that I didn't enjoy being with him. In fact the opposite of that was fast becoming my reality. But the whole thing was so awkward. I had no idea what was expected of me.

I groaned as I remembered I had promised Sabby she could come this time. Perhaps she could help take the heat off me. I suspected though, that Sabby would be pumping him for information on our time spent together.

I had a quick shower and changed back into jeans. Then I threw some clothes into my bag with my dream-catcher, left a note for Jared asking him to make sure my bed didn't get short-sheeted, and, with Scruffy trotting at my side, I headed down to the car park.

Grams was sitting at the kitchen table when I got home. She looked up from her porridge and said, 'Had enough?'

'I've got home study till next week.' I put some bread in the toaster.

'I see you've been bonding with the other students.' She rested a fingertip on her upper lip.

'Something like that. Tea?'

We were silent while I waited for the water to boil and the tea to brew. I filled her cup and placed it in front of her. She started as if only just realising I was there, and then she sighed and took a sip. 'So how's your Prince?'

It was my turn to sigh. 'You'll get to see him soon.'

He's coming here?' She jumped up from the table. 'Now?'

'No. On Saturday.'

'Oh.' She slumped back into her seat.

I studied her more intently. Her hair was silvery grey and she was wearing a beige tracksuit. Even Cyril's scales were beige.

'So what's up?' I asked.

She sighed again. 'It's Lionel.'

'Oh no.' I'd been so caught up in my own life I hadn't realised they had broken up. 'I'm sorry Grams.'

'He wants to get married.'

It took me a second to digest her words. 'What? But that's good, isn't it?'

'What's good about it?' She spooned some porridge into the air and let it dribble back into her bowl.

'Well, you get on really well.'

She nodded her head.

'You have heaps of common interests.'

'Like what?'

'You both love travelling.'

'That's true.' She stopped playing with her porridge and looked up at me.

'He's good looking and wealthy.'

The look on her face brightened. 'He is quite dashing.'

'And,' I had left the best till last, 'every other witch would be green with envy.'

'Not that that is important, but all the other witches *would* be jealous wouldn't they?'

'Grams they would cry themselves to sleep every night for the rest of their lives. I mean we are talking about The Weekly Witching News's Bachelor of the Year five years in a row.'

Her smile threatened to crack her face in two. You're right,' she said, 'Lionel and I were made for each other.' She flicked her wand and her hair turned bright orange. 'He's the man I've been waiting for my whole life.' Cyril raised his head to stare at Grams. His tongue stretched out towards her, tasting the air, and then his scales shimmered to orange.

'What about Grandpa?' Even though I'd never met the man (he'd died before Mum was born) I felt the need to stand up for him.

'Who?' she asked.

'Grandpa.' Honestly the woman had the attention span of a goldfish.

'Oh well, of course I loved him,' she said. 'And I'm sure that if he were still alive today we would be very happy.'

Mum appeared in the kitchen. 'Izzy.' She stared at my face for a second and then hugged me as if she hadn't seen me for a month. 'Oh thank goodness, you've managed to cheer her up.'

Grams picked up her plate and danced her way to the sink. She deposited the plate and then twirled on the spot, approaching Mum with a mischievous grin on her face. 'Guess what?' She held out her hands.

'What?' Mum eyed Grams' hands with a suspicious look on her face.

'You're going to have a new father.'

'I never knew my old one,' Mum said. 'Why do I need a new one?'

Grams burst out laughing and clapped her hands. 'Oh Prunella,' she said, 'be happy for me. Lionel and I are getting married.'

'Oh,' Mum said. 'Oh, Mother. That's wonderful.'

'I'm thinking a spring wedding,' Grams said.

I took that as my cue to start some homework.

***

I was surprised the next day when Mum called me down to the kitchen to find Aethan and Wilfred waiting for me. They looked incongruous in our kitchen, their warriors' clothes and bodies at odds with the cheery, yellow cabinets.

Aethan held a bunch of wildflowers in one hand. 'Here,' he said, thrusting them toward me.

'He picked them himself,' Wilfred said. 'I tried to help, but apparently mine weren't good enough.'

'You're not supposed to pull them out with the roots on them,' Aethan said. I wasn't sure, but it almost looked like he blushed.

Mum already had a vase out of the cupboard with water in it. 'They're lovely,' I said, arranging them in the vase.

'How are you feeling?' Aethan wiped his hands on the sides of his pants and then crossed them awkwardly in front of him.

'Excellent.' I raised my eyebrows and nodded towards Mum. She had moved into the lounge to give us some privacy but I was betting she was listening to every word.

Grandma Bella emerged from the hall to her rooms. Cyril perfectly matched the peacock green of her dress and shoes. She froze when she saw Aethan and Wilfred.

'Grams,' I said, 'come and meet my friends.'

She looked from us back to her rooms and licked her lips, turning as if to leave. But then she pasted a broad smile on her face and bustled towards us as I introduced her.

'Izzy didn't tell me she had an older sister,' Wilfred said as he bowed over her hand.

Grams giggled and fluttered her eyelashes at him. 'Oh young man,' she said, 'I bet you say that to all of your friends' grandmothers.'

'Only the ravishing ones.'

I rolled my eyes and turned to Aethan. 'Want to go for a walk?' I'd been studying all morning and was dying to get out of the house.

'Sure.' He held the door open for me and then followed me into the sunshine. The warm weather would hold for another few weeks yet and I wanted to enjoy as much of it as I could.

We wandered down the street towards the heart of the village.

'How old are you?' I asked Aethan.

'Twenty-one.'

Three years older than me. That was not so very much.

'So,' I said, 'what does being second-in-line to the throne entail?'

'When Orion takes the throne I'll be in charge of Isilvitania's defences.'

'Orion? Not Isla?'

He shook his head. 'The Faery Throne is passed down through the male line, unless there is no male. Then a female can ascend the throne.'

'That doesn't seem very fair. What does Isla think of that?'

He stopped walking and turned to face me. 'I must admit I'd never considered it.' He looked thoughtful for a moment and then shrugged a shoulder. 'It's the way it has always been.'

We were silent for a while as we continued to walk. 'What's Orion like,' I finally asked.

Aethan sighed. 'He's so serious. I worry about him.'

'All work and no play?'

'Something like that. He puts his position in front of everything, including his own happiness.'

'Isn't that the way of a monarch?'

Aethan bent and pulled a weed out of the footpath. He peeled one of the leaves off and threw it to the side. 'I guess so. It would be nice to think he could do his duty *and* be happy.'

'What about Isla? Is she happy?'

'Who knows what Isla is thinking. I like to believe she is not as shallow as she seems.'

I looked over at him, watching as he pulled the weed into pieces. 'Feel better?' I asked when he had finished.

'A little.' He grinned at me and I felt myself smiling back in response. 'Want to learn how to part the veils?' His question took me totally off guard.

'Part the veils?'

'What we do when we travel to and from Isilvitania.'

'Oh, yes, of course.' I hadn't realised how far we had walked. We were standing in front of the Eynsford Castle ruins.

'You can do it from anywhere,' he said, 'but this is near the heart of our land so it will be easier for your first time.'

I liked the way he said 'our' land a little too much. 'Will I be able to do it? I mean I am only half Fae.'

'I have no doubt you will. Your faery blood runs strong.' He pushed my hair behind my ears and stroked the top of one with a finger. A shiver ran down my spine. 'Although your ears aren't peaked. Come.' He led me off the path and down into the ruins. 'Now close your eyes and tell me what you can feel.'

He put his hands on my shoulders to steady me as I closed my eyes. His fingers burned through the thin cotton of my shirt as I craved his touch on my bare skin.

'What can you feel?' he asked.

I was *so* not telling him the truth. I shook my head and forced myself to concentrate. 'Ummm. Nothing.' I opened my eyes and looked at him. 'Perhaps I can't do it.'

He shook his head. 'You've only just begun trying. Close your eyes again.'

This time I reached out with all my senses except my sight. I could hear birds chirping and feel the breeze on my skin. The scent of fresh-cut grass made my nostrils tingle. As I relaxed my mind to my senses, a heaviness descended over me.

'I feel...,' How best to describe it? 'like someone put a blanket over me, but I can't *feel* the blanket, just the weight of it.'

Aethan squeezed my shoulders. 'Very good. That's the veil.'

I opened my eyes and the sensation dissipated. 'Really?' It lingered in the background and I realised it had always been there.

'Now to part it, you need to grasp it with your mind and then push it apart.' He reached out in front of him and moved his hands apart. For a second I could see the regal trees of Isilvitania. 'Now *you* do it.'

I closed my eyes again and let the weight settle over me, then I reached out with my hands and pushed. Nothing happened.

'You need to part it with your mind as well as your hands.'

I tried again. I could feel the thick fabric of the fog as it moulded itself to me. I reached out with my hands as I tore a hole with my mind, then I grabbed the edges and pushed them apart. I opened my eyes and there it was, Isilvitania.

'I did it.' I let go of the veil and flung my arms around Aethan a second before I realised what I was doing.

His body felt warm and hard as he wrapped his arms around me. It felt too nice by far, and I found myself wanting to stay like that forever. Instead I pulled back and looked up into his eyes. I hoped he wasn't annoyed.

He didn't look annoyed as he stared back at me. 'Well done.' His voice was low and husky.

Our faces were only a few inches apart and, glad I had managed to scrub off my moustache, I dropped my gaze to his full lips. It seemed a shame to be so close to them and not taste them.

I ached to feel his mouth on mine, to share his breath and feel his soul.

Kiss me. Oh please, kiss me.

'There you are.'

We jumped apart and turned to face Wilfred.

'Sorry,' he said, looking from Aethan to me, 'did I disturb something?' The amused look on his face told me he knew *exactly* what he'd disturbed.

'Aethan's teaching me to part the veils,' I said, wishing I couldn't feel my cheeks burning.

'Is that what he calls it?' Wilfred let out a chuckle.

Aethan punched him in the arm. 'We'd better get back.' He started to walk back to the road and I fought an urge to punch Wilfred as well. Talk about bad timing.

We walked back to the house in silence. I wasn't sure what they were thinking about but I was thinking about the 'almost' kiss. Would it have felt as amazing as the other night?

'Well, I'll see you Saturday,' I said when we got there.

'Saturday? What's on Saturday?' Wilfred asked.

'Oh, ahh, nothing,' Aethan said.

'I meant Monday,' I said. 'Don't know where my head is at.'

'Till Monday,' Aethan said.

They waited till I had closed the front door before leaving. Grams was nowhere to be seen, which in itself was strange. Why wasn't she there pumping me for information?

'Where'd Grams go?'

Mum was sitting in the lounge reading a book. A feather duster flitted around the room, and a broom swept the floor. 'Not sure. Perhaps she's gone to look at something for the wedding.'

Of course - the wedding. That's why she'd acted so weird. She was pre-occupied with wedding plans.

I picked up the vase of wildflowers and carried them up to my room, placing them on the only patch of my table not covered in notes and textbooks. Then I spent the next couple of hours pretending to study while in reality I daydreamed about Aethan.

***

'They're coming.' Sabina clapped her hands and turned from the window. She had arrived an hour ago to wait for the faeries to come.

'Oh goody.' As much as I tried, I couldn't force as much enthusiasm into my voice as she had in hers.

There was a knock on the front door then Mum called out, 'Isadora, you have company.' As if I didn't know.

I took a deep breath and shook my head. Why couldn't Aethan and I just go to the movies like normal people?

Sabina followed me down to the lounge where Aethan was waiting. He was dressed in his combat gear of furs and leather.

Oh great. In the green dress Sabina had picked out for me I looked ridiculously overdressed.

I heard Sabby catch her breath. 'Oh my.'

He did look very 'Oh my', with his muscles standing out on his arms and chest and his thick, dark hair highlighting the stubble on his cheeks. He picked up my hand and formally bowed his head over it. But as he stood back up, he shot me a cheeky grin.

For all his manliness, that grin was the thing that made my heart flutter the most. When he grinned at me like that, it was as if all pretences were gone. I could see the real him. He was no longer a Prince, no longer my teacher, just a man who might be interested in me as much as I was in him.

I introduced Sabina (who blushed and curtsied) and then I let Aethan take my arm upon his and lead me down to the field where the faery entourage waited.

It felt ridiculous. A total charade. And I'm sure that my Fae part, no matter what her relationship was like with Aethan in Trillania, would have agreed.

'How are you?' Aethan murmured once we had seated ourselves on the silk cushions.

'Better.' I was surprised how many days it had taken before the fatigue caused by my healing had gone.

I watched in amusement as Phantom and Scruffy tried to ignore each other. Scruffy had made overtures of friendship to Phantom (tried to sniff his butt), but for some reason Phantom had taken great offence at this (hissing and snapping), and they had each been pretending the other didn't exist since.

A familiar voice bellowed from the far side of the tent, 'Sorry I'm late.' Wilfred attempted to tiptoe through the piles of cushions and chattering Fae. I winced as he knocked over a goblet and tripped on the corner of a low table.

He plopped down onto a cushion next to Sabina. 'Well hello there.'

I shook my head and turned to Aethan. 'He found out?'

Aethan rolled his eyes and nodded.

'You're picturing me naked, aren't you?'

Sabina giggled. 'You are very hairy.'

'My mother was an orc.'

Sabby gasped and stifled another giggle. 'You're pulling my leg.'

'I'd like to. It's a very fine leg.'

There was a clapping of hands and then Isla, looking exquisite in a flowing, white dress, stood. 'If you remember last time we were here, Aethan promised us a poem.'

I resisted the urge to put my head in my hands. I had forgotten about the poem.

'What poem?' Sabby whispered.

I ignored her but Wilfred answered. 'Aethan's written Izzy a love poem.'

She let out a wistful sigh.

Isla continued mercilessly. 'Well Aethan, have you managed to craft your admiration for Isadora into a poem?' There was a silent challenge in the tone of her voice.

Aethan stood and pulled a piece of paper out of his vest pocket. 'I certainly have sister. It's not long, but I think you'll agree it is not the length of a poem but the content that is important.'

Oh Great Dark Sky. I cringed back into my cushion.

'Was up all night writing it,' Wilfred stage-whispered in Sabby's ear.

I had a moment to wish for a goblin attack before Aethan cleared his throat and began to read.

'Although there are many eyes of blue,
Yours are the prettiest I ever knew.
With your skin as pale as snow,

Only you make my heart glow.
From the moment we first met
Into my heart you have crept.'

He gave me an apologetic look and then sat back down, to a spatter of polite applause. 'I'm more of an action man than a poet.'

'I can see that.' I was torn between disappointment and relief that his poem hadn't been more flowery.

'That was rather poor Aethan.' Isla's face puckered into a frown. 'Surely Isadora means more to you than that.'

'How I feel about Isadora,' he stretched my name out into individual syllables, 'is my and her business.'

'I thought it was well done.' Wilfred's voice quavered with his attempt not to laugh.

'You joined the Border Guards didn't you?' Isla knelt beside me and cupped a hand around my cheek. 'How does a beauty like you spend your nights in the barracks?'

I wasn't sure what she was alluding to, and I didn't appreciate her question. I opened my mouth, without even thinking about what I was going to say, and all of a sudden I was caught up in spasm. Pain lanced through me, shaking me from side-to-side.

'Izzy.' I heard Sabby's cry of dismay, but couldn't answer her.

Wilfred and Aethan lowered me to a cushion where I thrashed and jerked.

'Close your mouth.' Aethan's voice was low but urgent.

I fixed my whole being on that single task, trying to regain control of my muscles. After a moment my lips closed together and the fit immediately stopped.

Scruffy whined and clambered onto my chest. 'I'm okay boy.' It hurt to talk and my voice rasped. He began to lick my face.

I had seen that. What I had just felt, I had seen it before.

Pieces of a puzzle clicked into place and suddenly I knew. I knew, and I felt my face burn with humiliation.

I had been right. This whole day was a sham.

When Queen Eloise had first accused Aethan of dating me he had tried to deny it. And he had had a fit. A fit just like the one I'd had.

So instead he had been forced into courting me.

That was why he hadn't kissed me at Eynsford Castle. That was why he hadn't wanted Wilfred to know about today. Embarrassment threatened to swallow me whole.

What I had just felt, what Aethan had felt that first day, was the Border Guard binding spell. He wasn't in love with me. He didn't want to spend more time with me. He just hadn't been able to tell his mother the truth. And now he was trapped into making everyone think he cared.

I had to end it. I had to end it now.

I pushed myself away from the cushions. 'Isla is correct.' I turned to stare at Aethan. 'I would have thought your *poem* would have been far more eloquent. Perhaps you need to rethink how you really feel about me.'

'Isadora.' I heard Mum's gasp from the other side of the marquee.

'Well I never,' Queen Eloise spluttered.

Aethan's face held the confusion he felt.

It went against every fibre of my being to be this rude. I had to do it for him. I had to do it for me.

'Perhaps, next time you court a woman you will put in more effort. After all,' I stood up and strode to the edge of the marquee, 'it's the little things that count.'

By the time I got back to my bedroom an ache had set up in my chest that rivalled my buffo burns.

He'd kissed me.

Sure it had been in the line of duty - but he'd *kissed* me. Like he'd meant it. Like he'd felt it. And for that brief moment my whole being had known him. Had known we were right for each other.

But it was all a lie.

It took them longer to turn up than I'd thought. Mum hovered in the doorway to my rooms while Sabby peeped over her shoulder.

'I don't want to talk about it.' I blew my nose and threw the tissue across the room towards the bin. I missed.

'I'm not quite sure what just happened,' Mum said. It was nice of her not to jump straight down my throat.

What to tell her? And how to say it without evoking the binding spell again?

A few more tears squeezed out of the corners of my eyes. Damn it. I didn't want to cry, it just made me feel more stupid. 'I realised I liked him more than he liked me.'

'So he's not very good at writing poetry.' Mum sat down on the edge of my bed.

I shook my head. 'It wasn't that.'

'Well what was it?'

I breathed out heavily. 'Mum, I'm sorry. I can't tell you.'

'Thomas was right?' Sabby asked. 'A secret cult?'

'It's not a cult.' I paused, half expecting the spasms again.

'Did they *do* something to you? If they did I'll, I'll…' Mum clenched her fists and stood. Her red face had a hard, determined look.

I placed a hand on her shoulder, pulling her back to the edge of the bed. I was going to have to change my tactic or blood would be shed. 'He's just not right for me.'

That was something she could understand. 'Oh. Okay then.' She sat for a minute while she contemplated my words. 'Well then, how about I make us a lemon cake?'

'With passionfruit icing?'

'Is there any other type?' She squeezed my knee as she hopped up, striding purposefully from the room.

'You're not going to tell me either?' Sabby fixed her large, green eyes on my face.

I shook my head. 'Sorry.'

'Oh well, at least I get cake.'

It was the simplest form of magic, but in the Scrumpleton household everything had always been fixable with a pot of tea and a slice of lemon cake.

I wished with all my heart that it were still that easy.

Chapter Twelve

Hell Hath No Fury Like A Woman Scorned

I'd managed to avoid Aethan all day, but the time was fast approaching when I had to head down to the sleep room. I wasn't looking forward to meeting his eyes. What would I see there?

I dilly-dallied long enough that the dungeon was already full when I arrived. I scanned the room hoping and dreading that he would be there.

Wilfred caught my eye and waved me over. 'Aethan said to go ahead. He'll be a few minutes late.'

He jumped onto a bed while I strapped on an armband. 'So he is coming?' I lay down on the bed next to him.

He lifted his head and stared over at me. 'Why wouldn't he?'

I shuffled a little to the side to give Scruffy more room. 'Oh no reason.' I mean *honestly*, was he not there on Saturday?

I screwed my eyes up, trying to squeeze the confused emotions out of me. Relief at his not being there, disappointment at his not being there. Relief he was coming, disappointment he was coming. I didn't know how much more I could take.

I was surprised when I stepped into Trillania. I hadn't thought I'd be able to sleep with that much energy running through me. Unfortunately it had all come with me. Confusion still reigned my thoughts.

'You're girlfriend's a hottie.'

It took me a second to realise Wilfred was talking about Sabina.

'Yep, she's cute.' I tried unsuccessfully to stop the next words from coming out of my mouth. 'Did Aethan think she was cute?'

Aghhhhh. Did I really say it?

'I don't know.' Wilfred seemed to be honestly considering my question. 'Did you?'

I spun around to see Aethan shimmering into view. 'Did I what?'

'Nothing?' I screeched, but Wilfred said, 'Think Izzy's friend was cute.'

Oh kill me. Just kill me now. Where was a goblin when you needed one?

'I must say, I didn't notice.'

Was he just saying that or was it the truth? Sabina was beautiful.

'Are we ready?' Aethan was acting as if there were nothing wrong. 'Tonight we're roaming. Rako's asked that we stay near Isilvitania. The Australian Guards have reported larger than normal numbers of goblins in Trillania.'

'Full moon?' Wilfred scratched his beard and looked at the sky. It was never fully dark in Trillania, but a full moon would still be visible.

'Not for another two weeks.'

Why was he acting as if nothing were wrong?

'Wonder what they're up to? They must have some sort of master plan.' I'd never seen Wilfred look so serious.

'They haven't had one of those since Santanas was dealt with.' Aethan turned his attention to me. 'I think you're ready to commute by yourself. We're going to travel to the woodland where we saw the garden faery.'

I was ready to commute alone? He didn't want to hold my hand.

I could feel the emotions swirling inside becoming more and more convoluted. Was he really that repulsed by me?

'Close your eyes and picture the woodland. Imagine yourself there. You imagining it?'

I nodded my head even though I wasn't even trying.

'Now picture yourself there.'

Aethan and Wilfred shimmered from view. I stayed exactly where I was. The relief at being alone was immediate.

It only lasted for a few seconds before Aethan reappeared. 'You didn't picture yourself there.'

'Sorry,' I mumbled.

Couldn't look him in the eye. Couldn't see what was there.

'Well come on.' He reached out his hand and clasped mine.

I jerked it away, stumbling to the side. 'You don't have to do this,' I said.

'Do what?'

'Be so nice to me.' I shook my head.

'Ahhhhh.' He ran a hand through his hair. 'Is this about Saturday?'

'Don't worry, I worked it out.'

I couldn't believe I had been stupid enough to believe someone like *him* could have been interested in me. The humiliation rose like a high tide, threatening to drown me.

'Izzy.' He reached out and took my hand again. 'Don't do this.'

I stared at my feet.

He tugged on my hand. 'Look at me.'

I lifted my eyes to his knees, then his waist. Up his chest to his neck. I stopped there for a second before propelling them the last few inches. I stared into the depths of those eyes and soaked in what I saw.

Concern tinged with… what was that? Was it pity?

I ripped my hand out of his and spun, running towards the trees.

'Izzy.' I could hear him coming after me.

'I can't,' I gasped. 'I can't.' My heart pounded erratically. My lungs laboured to bring in air.

The shame. Oh, the *shame*. It was too much.

What did he think of me, so keen to have him court me? So happy to have his attention.

'Izzy.' He was gaining on me.

I couldn't let him catch me. Couldn't look into those glorious eyes and see what he really thought.

He was right behind me, his hand brushing my arm as he tried to grab me. I had to get away. I closed my eyes and pictured myself anywhere. Anywhere but there.

The sound of him disappeared and I opened my eyes. Trees crowded around me on all sides. Nightmare Forest. I thought of the buffos, and the slug-like monster I'd seen in my memory and I willed myself away.

This time when I opened my eyes I was by the sea. Salt air pushed my hair off my face. That was more like it. Now I could pretend the water on my cheeks was from the ocean.

I sat on a rock and stared out to sea. The water emulated my mood. Dark and stormy. The wind swirled around me, tugging at my clothes. My feelings swirled inside me, knotting to a hard ball. The pressure was unbearable. I had to do something to release it.

I pictured myself in my war uniform. The fur of the vest was soft against my skin, the leather snug. I strapped daggers to the outside of my thighs and sheathed a sword across my back. I conjured up a bow and a quiver full of arrows.

A mount. I needed a mount. For tonight a horse would not do. I needed something stronger, faster, *more dangerous.*

Without knowing what I did, I sent out my mind and scoured the land until I felt her. There. In the north.

Come, I called, *tonight we hunt.*

I felt a pressure on my mind, powerful and curious.

Come, I commanded.

Her deep-green scales gleamed almost black in the light of the stars as long sweeps of her wings propelled her at breakneck speeds. Her shadow stained the ground beneath her as she raced towards me. She threw her head back and let out a roar, then slowed to circle lazily overhead.

She was magnificent in her maleficence. Talons like steel. Teeth like spears. Her sinuous body covered in armour. She fluttered her massive wings as she craned her neck down to stare at me with glittering, intelligent eyes. Then she snapped her wings to her side and dropped soundlessly from the sky, landing in front of me like a cat.

Those eyes bore into mine, testing me, probing me. I stood straight and strong and willed her to do what I commanded. I willed her to be mine.

Finally she shook her head and rustled her wings, lowering herself to the ground. I climbed onto a wing, making my way up her armoured body to the base of her long, scaly neck. Steam curled out of her nostrils as she watched me sit.

Once I had my thighs clasped tight, I raised an arm and pointed at the sky. 'Fly,' I shrieked.

She ran awkwardly; one hop, two hops. I jerked in my seat. And then she stretched her wings out to the sides and thrust them down. We swept into the air, rocking gently between each flap of those massive limbs.

I had to do something with my cacophony of feelings.

Someone had to pay. Someone had to suffer. And I knew just whom those somebodies were going to be.

I leant forward in my seat as we raced across the sky, and I scoured the land for goblins.

***

For a while all I saw were dreamers; dreamers with the occasional Border Guard skulking surreptitiously in the shadows. The dreamers were unaware of our passing, but the Border Guards clutched their weapons as our shadow darkened them.

But I had other game to chase. I pictured Isilvitania in my mind and pushed it out to Emerald. She snorted a stream of fire and changed course. The sky wavered and where clouds had been, only stars shone.

I felt a surge of triumph as my power boiled inside me. They were here. I urged Emerald to the left and lay forward onto her neck.

Fire. In the distance. We sped towards it. A low wooden structure attached to Isilvitania castle was in flames and goblins and guards fought in its light. The clash of their weapons reached me over the noise of the wind.

Bands of orcs attempted to scale the walls of the castle, and a couple of trolls lumbered through the trees. There were so many goblins. Too many for the Guard to handle. What were they all doing here?

A group of dreamers played cricket on the green while more looked on. They were oblivious to the fighting going on around them. A troll lumbered from the trees with a huge club dangling from his hand. He surveyed the players while he tossed his weapon from hand-to-hand.

Emerald and I flew over the top of the melee, banking in a wide arc back towards it. My skin felt ripe, ready to burst as the power arced inside. I drew it out, wrapping it around me like a cloak, and then we attacked.

Emerald lowered her head and swept her wings back as she dived towards the ground. She let out a stream of fire as we roared past the orcs. I hooked my feet behind a couple of her scales and knelt on her neck, fitting an arrow to my bow.

Flaming orcs fell from the castle walls, shining like beacons in the half-lit night. I released my arrows with a breath of power, speeding them towards the troll. They lodged in his neck and he dropped his club, looking around in bewilderment.

'Dragon,' one of the dreamers screamed, pointing into the sky. The rest of them stopped their game and stared open-mouthed at Emerald. They stood like that for a few seconds before the adrenaline hit their blood stream. You could tell when it kicked in because half of them started screaming hysterically and running towards the woods and the other half just disappeared.

Oh great. Totally unaware of an army of goblins and a big, fat troll, but throw a dragon into the mix and they got all hysterical.

I was *so* going to hear about this from Rako.

Emerald banked again and attacked from the other side. I could see the goblins, some attacking Border Guards and others chasing terrified dreamers through the trees, and my anger expanded exponentially.

Arrows weren't going to be very effective at the speed we were going. I knew I had lucked in with the troll. And even though Emerald's fiery breath was a deadly weapon, it wasn't enough.

I reined her in with some pressure from my knees and she hovered, the flapping of her wings fanning the fire to a new height.

I took all my humiliation, all my sorrow and I channelled them into my anger. I pointed at a goblin pursuing a woman in a baby-blue night dress. 'Take that,' I screeched.

Even *I* got a fright when the lightning bolt lanced from my fingertips. It pierced his chest and he dropped to his knees and then toppled to the ground.

Border Guards and goblins alike stared up at Emerald and me. I recognised Jared and one of his trainers, Brent. Isgranelda had a look of shock on her face as she shielded her eyes from the fire and gazed at me. A dark slash coloured her right cheek. Then her mouth curled into a triumphant smile and she threw back her head and laughed.

A goblin lifted a crossbow and fired it towards us. Emerald hissed as it bounced off her scales. She reached out her neck to blast fire onto him. He shrieked in pain and dropped to the ground, rolling over and over.

'Izzy.' Aethan dashed from the trees and waved his bow at me. 'What are you doing?'

What was I doing? I was damned well saving their arses, that's what.

Another bolt slammed into Emerald, wedging in the soft tissue under her arm. She bellowed in pain and flapped higher into the sky.

Leave, I said into her mind.

More bolts followed. One nicked the side of her neck, spraying black blood over me.

'Go,' I yelled at her.

She shook her head and snarled; spitting fire and fighting against my mental command. Anger won out. Her roar resounded off the walls of the castle as she nose-dived towards the goblins.

Bolt after bolt slashed towards her. Some bounced harmlessly, but others buried themselves deep between her scales. Fire poured out of her and over them, but still they shot.

'Stop,' I screeched, pulling back on her neck.

A bolt lodged into her belly and she let out a huffing grunt. She turned to stare at me and then eyed an arrow that was wedged in her neck.

Help me. Her silent command boomed into my mind, almost blasting me from her back.

I shuffled up her neck while she wheeled in the sky. 'Fine,' I said, 'we'll go out together.' She snorted her approval as I worked the arrow from under her scale, and I wasn't sure if it were for the relief from some of her pain, or for my mental image of us going out in a blaze of glory.

This time as we approached, the Border Guard stopped its forward attack and danced away from the goblins. Emerald sent her fire into the gap they had provided, flambéing the entire front row of goblins.

Lightning danced from my fingers as I speared warrior after warrior. Laughter bubbled on my lips and I threw back my head and let out a triumphant shout.

A troll smashed into the back of the Border Guard, swinging his club and arms with equal effect. He lifted them bodily into the air, tossing them aside like rag dolls.

Emerald raced into the sky, spinning as she went. Higher and higher she climbed, pushing me back against her shoulders. I clasped my limbs around her neck and prayed. Finally she turned, swooping back towards the earth.

If I had thought she had gone fast before it was nothing compared to what she did now. With her wings tucked in and her neck stretched out straight, the wind whipped over us. I pressed my face against her scales and exulted in the feel of the speed.

At the last second her wings popped out and she levelled out much lower than I had thought possible. Reaching out with those cruel talons she plucked the troll into the air. She ripped him into two chunks and threw the pieces at the goblins. Blood and gore spattered them.

On her next pass she did the same to a goblin, ignoring the cross bolt arrows as she ripped his head off with her teeth.

Anger coiled in her, lashing out at her enemy. It flowed through her and over me, and for that time we were one; our aims identical, our needs identical, we tore our way through the goblin ranks.

She was bleeding from a dozen puncture wounds but I thought she was infallible. And then, as she levelled out for a pass, a bolt struck the front of her wing. A million-in-one shot, it nicked the webbing, tearing through the membrane to the middle bone.

Shrieking, she pivoted to the side. The wing no longer held us aloft. I screamed and wrapped myself around her neck as we crashed through the trees, hurtling through branches and trunks and limbs until we slammed against the bole of a large oak.

'Emerald.' I climbed shakily off her neck and crawled to her head. 'Emerald.' Please don't let her be dead.

She opened one enormous eye and stared at me. An image of us in a blaze of glory flashed into my mind. Then her eye slid shut and her mind was gone.

'Oh Emerald.' I wrapped my arms around her head, blinking tears onto her.

Warm air from her nostrils moved against my arm and a picture of a mouse playing dead flashed through my mind, quickly followed by a simple command. *Fight.*

I stood and turned in time to see the goblins. They approached warily. I reached for my power but it had disappeared during the crash. I raised my hands defensively, and they stopped.

How long before they realised I was bluffing? I only had to hold them off until the Guard got there.

'She's over there,' Wilfred roared.

'Get her.' It was a female voice, thick and accented. 'Take her now.'

One of the goblins darted towards me. I grabbed my sword from its sheath on my back and slashed at his hand.

A female goblin? All of the ones I had ever seen had been men.

He danced back out of reach and I heard the sound of fighting coming towards me. Just a few more moments and I would be safe.

'Take her or suffer my wrath.'

At her voice the goblin warriors swarmed towards me. I managed to wound a couple of them before they overwhelmed me. Strong arms grasped me and prised the sword from my fingers. I could hear Wilfred yelling and Aethan calling my name. But they were too late.

The world shimmered, fading from view as the goblins took me captive.

Chapter Thirteen

Uhh Ohh!!!

'Well, well, well, what have we here?' She had a strong, proud voice.

The goblins held my arms tight and turned me to face her. As tall as me, she had dark skin and black, dreadlocked hair that fell to her waist. Her clothing was made of leather, adorned with teeth and bones.

She reached out her finger and dabbed at a cut on my shoulder. Her finger came away smeared red. She popped it into her mouth, sucked it clean, and said, 'That was easy.'

'Who are you?' I tried to keep the shaking out of my voice, but failed miserably.

Her smile revealed teeth filed to a point. It wasn't a nice smile. 'I'm Galanta.'

Galanta the Goblin Queen? '*The* Galanta?' I said.

'Oh goody, you've heard of me.' She polished her long, black talons on her leather vest.

'To what do I owe the pleasure?'

She stopped polishing her nails and looked up, holding my gaze with her eerie, black eyes. A ring of red around the outside of her iris took that eerie and amplified it to freaky.

'I want to chat.' Her guttural voice ruined the innocence of the statement.

'About what?'

'You, and the second-in-line to the Fae crown.'

'Aethan? What about him?'

'I heard it on the apple vine that you had broken up.'

'You mean grapevine,' I said.

'I said apple vine and I meant apple vine.'

'Apples don't grow on vines.'

Her face took on a steely look and she stalked towards me.

'Okay, apple vine,' I said.

She snapped her teeth together and visibly restrained herself. 'Is it true or not?'

'We were never really dating.' What the hell was it to her?

'But you love him?'

'No.' I said it *way* too quickly.

She snorted. 'So you *do* love him.'

'No I don't.' I didn't love him, damn it. So why could I feel my face turning red?

'I won't tell anyone.' Her face took on a conspiratorial look. It didn't suit her at all. 'I just want to hear it from the pygmy's mouth.'

'You mean the horse's mouth?'

For a split second her face showed black rage. It was gone so quickly I almost thought I'd imagined it.

'Ahhhh. So you don't mind swearing that you won't marry him.'

This was getting *way* too weird. 'I won't what?'

'Marry him.'

'What's it to you?'

'If you don't love him, what's it to you?' She stalked towards me and ran a finger down my cheek. I jerked my head away from her, pulling against the restraints of her guards. Her finger dug deeper, her sharp nail tearing at my skin.

And *that* was when I remembered I could leave anytime I wanted. 'Well it's sure been a pleasure,' I said, 'but it's time to be going.' I shut my eyes and willed myself away. The pressure on my arms remained and I opened my eyes to the same situation I'd been in.

Galanta had an amused look on her face. 'Going somewhere?' She threw back her head and laughed.

'What have you done?'

'I drank your blood. Now you are mine. Come,' she gestured to her warriors. 'Things are about to get interesting.'

I was guessing her idea of interesting was quite different to my own. I fought them as hard as I could. Throwing myself from side-to-side and flailing my arms, but I may as well have been a babe for all the good it did.

They dragged me out of the woods, into a small clearing. A bonfire blazed at one end of it, a stake stood at the other. They pulled my arms behind me and tied them around the stake.

Oh Great Dark Sky. This was not good at all. Where were Aethan and Wilfred when I needed them?

Drums started to bang; the pace slow and steady as goblins chanted and moved in a lurching dance around the large fire. Sweat dribbled down my body as the heat scorched my skin.

The lurching and chanting increased in tempo as the goblins picked up the drum beat. Faster and faster they whirled around the fire, the slapping of their feet resonating with the throbbing of the drums.

If only I could reach my powers. I closed my eyes and willed them to come to me. They may as well have been non-existent. It was *so* frustrating. My witch powers were almost useless. And what I had begun to recognise as my faery powers, came upon me when I least expected them, seemingly with the sole purpose of destroying goblins. Well here I was, desperately in need of some goblins being destroyed and what did I have? Big, fat nothing.

Trying not to cry, I sagged back against the post.

The drums, banging and beating so harshly one second, were totally still the next. Knowing that whatever they had stopped for had something to do with me, made the silence that followed harsher than the chanting had been.

I tried to blow a piece of hair that was tickling my cheek off my face but it was stuck to my sweat. A hand with long black talons appeared in front of me and gently removed the hair.

'Is that better?' Galanta asked.

'Yes thank you.' She had me where she wanted me. Angering her didn't seem like such a good idea.

'It's the little things that make the difference,' she purred. Her long, pointy teeth belied the kindness of her words.

I started to feel ill. What was she planning to do to me?

'Now be a good girl and say it.'

Was she *still* going on about the marriage thing? 'No.'

'It's just a few words.'

I had no idea what she was going to get out of this, but if she got *anything* it was too much. 'Nope.'

'Poor Isadora.' She rolled the 'r' making it sound European. 'So loyal, so young, so brave.' She walked around the stake, trailing a finger around my body as she went. 'Are you really willing to die for this?'

I didn't want to die for it. It was stupid, I knew. They were just words. And we were never going to get married. But the stubborn part of me had stepped in, and now there was no going back.

'It's such a little thing.' She pouted at me. 'All you've got to do is promise that you won't marry him.'

I shook my head.

'She's blonde you know,' she continued. 'It turns out that brunettes aren't his thing after all.'

I closed my eyes as a vision of Aethan entwined with a busty blonde danced into my head. Was it the same one he had lip-locked a few years ago?

'Just say it and all of this will go away.' Her voice had become hypnotic, lulling me with its cadence and lilt. 'Then we can be friends.'

My eyes snapped open. I may not have known if what she said about Aethan were true, but I knew for sure that she and I would never be bosom buddies.

'Now Galanta,' I said, staring into her cold, black eyes. 'You and I both know that that's *never* going to happen.'

She snarled at me, shaking her head like a lion. 'So young, so stupid.' She pulled her dagger out of the holster on her belt, walking over to the fire to hold the end of the blade in the flames.

Oh that *so* did not look good.

When it was red hot she came back to me and waved it in front of my face. I noticed her warriors had gathered in a semi-circle to watch. If I hadn't been worried before, I certainly was now. Now I was shit scared.

'Sure you don't want to change your mind?' she said, reaching out and lifting up my shirt. 'While the cats are away the dogs will play.'

'It's mice you bitch.' I gritted my teeth and braced for the pain.

Growling, she pressed the tip of the burning knife to the soft skin of my stomach. I could feel skin blistering and smell hair burning and I screamed the loudest scream I'd ever heard. By the time she pulled the knife away I was emotionally and physically exhausted, and I knew the fun had only just begun. Panting, I hung from the stake, trying to think my way through this rationally.

Why did she want me to say it?

Galanta wandered back to the fire to reheat her knife and then she returned. She smiled hideously at me and then seared the knife into the other side of my gut. My shriek cut through the air as I felt the scorching pain. Even when she stopped, the burning went on. I could hear my breath panting in hoarse sobs.

What harm would it do to say it? It was just a few words.

I screamed and shuddered as she burnt me. My whole body was on fire. She worked her way down my arms and my legs, then across my back. But I couldn't say it. The words refused to come out of my mouth.

The pain overwhelmed me, threatening my sanity. I dived inwards to the soft cocoon of my core, where it was muffled and distant. The golden pools of my mind glowed around me and suddenly, I knew what to do.

I hung onto one of those pools and with my remaining strength forced myself back to consciousness. The pain flared brightly in my mind. I forced it to the side and allowed pure rage to control me. Dipping into that golden pool I pictured the bindings falling free from my hands. They slithered away and piled at my feet.

With my arms still behind me, I imagined the cruellest weapon I could visualise; a short sword with three jagged blades emerging from the handle. Each blade was designed to do more damage coming out than going in.

I waited till she approached me again and let her press the blade to my skin. Then I whipped my hand around and plunged the dagger into her side.

Her eyes widened in disbelief as I wrenched it from her. The blade tore at organ and muscle.

I dipped my fingers into her blood and placed them in my mouth. Gagging, I forced myself to swallow the cloying, slimy liquid.

Her blood tingled as it entered my body, and her control began to fade. I just needed a few more seconds and then I would be free.

She staggered away from me, stumbling to her knees. Roaring in fury, her warriors raced towards her; towards me. But they were too late.

As a warrior reached out a hand to grasp my hair I closed my eyes and shimmered back to where I'd entered Trillania.

Emerald. I sent out a mental call. I had to know if she were alive.

Her answer came from the direction of the Black Mountains. It was faint and tinged with pain. It was my fault she was injured. I had to help her. But there was no way I was going to be able to do it like this.

I sagged to the ground, trying to ignore the burning of my skin. I wasn't sure how the whole faery-me, witch-me thing worked, but I had to hope I could use it to my advantage.

'I hope you can hear me,' I rasped. 'I'll take the pain and you help her.' This had to work, it *had* to. The worst part was that I wouldn't know if it had.

I closed my eyes and willed myself back. As soon as my spirit touched my body the wounds of my mind transferred themselves. Pain lanced through me and I gasped awake.

Chaos ruled the room. Scruffy was on the end of my bed with his head thrown back. Howls of loss ripped from his throat. Guards stood in clusters talking animatedly. Rako waved his arms as he yelled at Aethan. 'Two of them? How could you let them take two of them?'

I ignored them all as I reached a hand to unclasp my arm band.

Have to do this. Have to help.

Pain lashed my every move. Blisters burst and fluid trickled down my arms as I struggled with the catch, my swollen fingers too stiff to manage it.

'She's awake.'

Can't lose focus. Have to succeed.

Aethan's face, creased with worry, came into view. He winced as he looked at me. 'What happened?'

I shook my head and motioned to the band.

Have to get it off.

He reached over and unclipped the latch, gently opening the band and taking it off. It was the only patch of smooth, unbroken skin on my arm.

I gasped with relief and lay back. He undoubtedly thought I didn't want to risk going back to Trillania. He didn't know I had every plan of going back. At least I hoped I was going to.

Go to her.

I closed my eyes and let the pain wash over me, hanging onto it with every fibre. I drew it in till it consumed me. Red spun in front of my eyes and I let it drag me down towards unconsciousness. I hoped she could access Trillania from there. It was the closest thing to sleep I could give her.

Down, down through a void of black; agony smothering my every thought. I spun slowly in the dark, clinging to the pain, and I waited for her return.

***

The room was the same as it had been the last time I'd opened my eyes. Scruffy still howled, guards still milled and Rako still waved his arms and yelled. But now my body was covered in an icy, wet towel.

I could see another figure lying on one of the other beds, but the rest were empty.

I moaned as pain danced across my mind. Scruffy immediately stopped howling, whimpering instead as he licked my foot.

'Hey boy,' I whispered. Even *that* hurt my throat.

'How are you?'

I tried not to move my head as I rolled my eyes to Aethan's. 'My own fault.' The physical pain trivialised my emotions, and suddenly, I felt very stupid.

I had alerted dreamers to my presence. I had almost got Emerald killed. I had let myself get captured and tortured. There was no excuse for any of it, and I was ashamed of my behaviour.

He shook his head. 'No it was…'

Before he could finish his sentence, my Mum's voice cut through the rest of the noise.

'Where is she?' I'd heard Mum angry before but I had never heard her like this. Rage shook her voice as she swept into the room. 'What have you done to her?'

Oh whizbang. This was *so* not good. She hadn't wanted me to join and now she was going to see me like this.

Her eyes lighted on me and she let out a gasp. She pushed Border Guards aside as if they were half their size as she made her way to my bed. 'What have they done?'

'I'm okay,' I croaked. Oh yeah, *that* was convincing.

'You are most certainly *not.*' Her voice cracked like a whip on the 'not' and I winced. She pulled the edge of the towel back and tears filled her eyes. 'My baby,' she said. 'Oh my baby.' She whirled and stalked back to Rako. 'Did you do this to her?' Her finger poked his chest with each word.

'I can assure you Ma'am that this was not done by our hands.'

'Then by whom?' She glared around the room.

'Goblins.' I managed to make my voice loud enough for her to hear. 'It was goblins.'

'May I ask how you knew?' Rako asked.

'Half an hour ago her familiar appeared in my kitchen, howling and crying. I could only surmise that something terrible had happened to Isadora. I see now I was correct.' Her voice still trembled with rage.

'Your daughter is a hero,' Rako said. 'She single-handedly turned a battle against a horde of goblins attacking Isilvitania.' I noted he didn't mention anything about my dragon mount.

Mum shot me a look of pride but her back was still stiff. 'That doesn't explain why she is like this.'

'She was captured and tortured.'

Tears started to pour down Mum's cheeks. 'Why haven't you healed her?'

'I can't.' Brinda's voice came from behind me. 'It would take too much of her energy to heal so large an area. She could die.'

'You must be able to do something.'

'I am removing the heat from the burns. Then I will place a dressing on them.'

I was going to look like a mummy if she had to bandage all my burns. 'Scars?' I whispered. I could feel some welts on my face that I didn't remember receiving.

'My dressing will prevent scarring.'

'I want her brought home,' Mum said. 'You will tend her wounds there, and then this madness will stop.' She waved her arm around her as she spoke. 'No more Border Guards.'

What? I struggled to sit up but Aethan pushed gently on my shoulders, pinning me to the bed.

'I think that is up to Isadora.' Rako's voice was stiff.

Mum turned her attention to me. 'No more, Isadora. Surely you can see now that this is too dangerous.'

I didn't say anything and she took my silence for acquiescence. That was a fight I would leave till I was better. There was no *way* I was leaving the Guard. I had to get even with that bitch Galanta.

'What happened to this girl?' She waved an arm at the other bed and I realised it was Isgranelda lying there. The snippet of conversation I'd heard earlier made sense. They'd captured two of us.

'I gave her a sleeping potion,' Brinda said into the silence of the room. 'She had a headache.'

'This is a rather odd infirmary,' Mum said. 'Why do you arrange the beds like this?'

'We find it helps with the healing if they are able to engage each other.' Brinda was doing a good job of masking the real purpose of the room, but my mind was on other things.

What had happened to Isgranelda? Was she dead? I hadn't liked her at all, but it didn't mean I wanted to see her dead.

As if on cue Isgranelda moaned. So, not dead then. Brinda rushed to her side.

'She's bleeding,' Mum said. 'Why is she bleeding?'

Not dead, but wounded.

'Get her out of here,' Rako yelled, waving an arm in our direction.

Aethan wheeled my bed towards the door. 'Prunella,' he said, 'we will take Isadora home now.'

'But why is she bleeding?'

Aethan maintained his silence on the subject. He wouldn't have been able to explain it without suffering the effects of the binding spell. After a while Mum let out a huff and stopped asking. I'm not sure who was more pleased, Aethan or me.

They moved me oh-so-carefully off the bed and onto a litter, but even that caused me to shriek in pain. Then they placed the litter in the back of a car and drove me to Eynsford. Another painful transfer from the litter to my bed, and I was home.

Mum huffed and puffed as she bustled around me. She carefully spread ice over my towel and I even managed to sleep for a while as the cold stilled the pain.

Brinda arrived hours later and she and Mum removed the towel and dressed the wounds. Mum stared at my burns with a look of hard resolve. It was going to be difficult to tell her I was going back.

I waited till she had gone to the kitchen to get more ice and whispered, 'Isgranelda?'

'Alive,' Brinda said. 'It was touch and go for a while there. She was pretty badly wounded.' She reached over me and hung a dream-catcher on the bed head.

I nodded my head, partly in thanks for the dream-catcher, and partly in response to the information, and closed my eyes. The salve felt wonderful on my skin.

'I will have to do this every day for two weeks,' Brinda said.

'Two weeks?' I couldn't bear the thought of being stuck in bed for two weeks. I had to find Galanta and kill her.

'Two weeks,' she replied, her voice firm with authority.

Rako waited till I was well enough to sit up in bed before he visited. Mum showed him into my room, her face stony with anger. Her feelings on my returning had not softened with time, and I hadn't summoned up the courage yet to tell her.

Rako waited till she left the room before he spoke. 'You are healing?'

Too nervous to speak, I nodded my head. Was he here to kick me out of the Guard?

'How did they capture you?'

'I forgot I could disappear, and then by the time I remembered she had done something with my blood.'

'She drank it?'

'I wouldn't go that far, but yes, she consumed some.'

'A blood bond.' He scrubbed his fingers through his stubble. 'What did she want?'

'She wanted me to say I wouldn't marry Aethan.' I said it as fast as I could, but it was no less embarrassing.

He started to chuckle, his laughter slowly dying off as he realised I wasn't laughing with him. 'You're serious?'

'Deadly serious.'

'And did you?'

I squirmed. 'No.'

'Why ever not?'

'I didn't know why she wanted me to say it, and I felt it best not to give her what she wanted.'

'You thought the words might give her some kind of power?'

'Well after the whole blood thing I didn't know what they would give her.'

Black shadows hung under his eyes. He looked like he hadn't slept for days. 'What is she up to?' he murmured to himself. He looked up at the ceiling while he thought. 'How did you get away,' he finally asked.

'I managed to tap into my powers. I stabbed her and tasted her blood.' I screwed my face up at the memory of the foul stuff.

'Clever girl.' Coming from Rako, that was quite a compliment.

He stood up as if he were about to leave and then stopped and stared at the photo of Grams and Mum on my bedside table. 'Might I take another copy of that?' he asked. 'I seem to have misplaced the other one. I was sure I put it into your file.'

I watched while he copied the photo again. 'So that's it?' I finally said.

'What do you mean?'

'You're not going to yell at me for riding a dragon?'

He rubbed at an eye for a moment and then sat back down. 'You are bonded to her. What is there for me to say?'

'You're not going to yell at me for scaring those dreamers or leaving Aethan and Wilfred… what did you say? Bonded?' I stared at him. 'That's not the first time I rode Emerald is it?'

He shook his head. 'You've been bonded for a while now.'

'Why won't anybody tell me these things? Why won't you tell me about what I've been doing when I'm dream-walking?' My voice rose with my frustration. I clenched my fists into the bedspread in an attempt to calm myself.

'We can't tell you lass.' His voice was kind. 'If we changed your perception of a memory you may not get it back.'

I opened my mouth to argue but I didn't know what to say.

'What if I told you about something that had happened that I'd thought was funny, not realising that the same event had made you sad. Your perceived memory is now one of hilarity; it wouldn't match the real one. You would either remember it differently or wouldn't remember it at all.'

'But just one memory, surely it wouldn't matter.'

'What if you'd made a major decision based on how sad that event had made you feel? A huge, life-changing decision.'

The enormity of what he was telling me sunk in. It could alter my past and therefore, also, my future. It could change who I was.

'Don't tell me anything.' I shook my head vigorously. 'I don't want to know.'

Chapter Fourteen

Three Blind Mice

'Only a few more days and I'll be able to go back,' I said to Sabby. My wounds had healed to faint-pink patches.

'You're crazy,' she said. 'Why would you go back to that?' Before I could say anything she added, 'I don't know why you're bothering with him.'

'What *are* you talking about?'

'*You* know who I'm talking about.' She placed her hands on her hips and stared at me. 'I mean he hasn't even been to visit you.'

I wasn't sure if I were pleased about that or not. I still cringed whenever I thought about my behaviour. 'He's not the reason I'm going back.'

'It doesn't matter,' she said. 'I'm not going to tell you.'

'Tell me what?' Whizbang, could she get any weirder?

'Nothing.' She sat back down and twiddled her fingers for a few seconds before saying, 'Oh fine.' She flicked her wand at her handbag and an envelope rose from one of the pockets and floated to her. She plucked it out of the air and handed it to me.

Her name was inscribed in gold writing on the front, and the back had a broken wax seal. I pulled a piece of paper out and unfolded it, running an eye down the elegant script.

It was an invitation for the following evening to a ball at Isilvitania. It was being held in honour of Aethan's birthday. 'Oh.' I put it carefully down on the coffee table.

'Oh's about right,' Sabina said. 'While you've been convalescing he's been planning a ball.'

'None of my business.' I hadn't got an invitation. Where was my invitation?

'Rumour has it that his mother is trying to find him a wife.' She really wasn't helping with my attempts to remain calm.

'Are you going?' I was rather proud of my ability to keep my voice level.

She blushed and looked away.

'Please tell me you are. I need someone to get all the gossip for me.'

'All right then,' she huffed like she was doing me the biggest favour in the world. 'But only because you insist.'

***

I was lying in the loungeroom, trying to take my mind off the ball by reading a book. I wasn't doing a very good job of it. I'd been staring at the same page for an hour.

They would have started arriving by now. All the single women wearing beautiful gowns, designed to catch Aethan's eye. Even though I knew there was nothing between us, I still felt ill at the thought.

I had fallen for him, *damn it,* and it seemed there was nothing I could do about my feelings except ignore them.

I heard footsteps leading up to the front door and then Grams' voice telling Eric to let her in. She had been off with Lionel looking for a wedding venue.

'Why aren't you ready for the ball?' She placed her suitcase by the door and gave me a hug.

'You had to get an invitation,' I said, returning to my slovenly position in the armchair.

'That's ridiculous, of course you would have been invited.'

'Grams, I dumped him. I think that would have been when my invitation got torn up.'

'You could be right about that,' she said.

'Where's Mum?' I asked. It wasn't like her not to be home in the evening.

'Probably *book club,*' Grams said with a mischievous grin on her face.

'Book club?'

'That's what she calls it, but have you ever seen her reading a book?'

'She was reading one last week.'

'Huh.' Grams sat down in the chair opposite me. 'Maybe she really did join a book club. I was hoping it was code for something naughty.'

A knock at the door interrupted us. I hopped up and opened it, secretly hoping it was a last-second invitation to the ball. It wasn't. Instead, a pumpkin, a rat, and six white mice sat on the doormat.

'Grams,' I said, 'you've got to see this.'

'I don't believe it,' she said in amusement when she peered out the door.

'What is it?' I asked.

'Well, I've only ever read about it, but it looks like someone has cast a Cinderella spell.'

'A what?'

'A Cinderella spell.' She clapped her hands together. 'I've always wanted to see one in action.' She backed away from the door, watching me with an excited look on her face. 'Izzy,' she said, 'they've come to take you to the ball.'

'Oh, no they haven't.' If I hadn't been formally invited there was no *way* I was turning up. I couldn't shut the door though, because the pumpkin, which I was sure had not moved, was blocking it.

'You can't fight it,' Grams said. 'Just go with the flow.'

'I am not going to let a pumpkin publicly humiliate me.'

A green shoot emerged from the top of the pumpkin, winding its way through the air towards me.

A sharp knife would fix that. I turned and ran for the kitchen. A step short of the knife block the pumpkin vine wound around my ankle. I reached down and pulled it off but it immediately re-attached to the other leg. 'Let go,' I said as another creeper emerged from the vegetable. It grew at an alarming rate, reaching out to snag my other leg. The two vines tugged together, whipping my feet out from under me and pulling me to the ground.

'Best not to fight it Izzy.' Grams rubbed her hands together.

'Like hell.' The thought of being dragged off to that ball leant me the strength of ten men as I wrestled with the vines. But the pumpkin kept throwing more and more creepers at me until finally I was encased in green foliage from head to foot. 'You have got to be kidding.'

'What's that Izzy?' Grams said. 'Your voice is all muffled.'

'What's going on?' I yelled.

'I'd say it's dressing you.'

I lay still, trying not to panic as claustrophobia tried to claim me. A warm tingling started at my head and worked its way down to my feet. When it had dissipated, the vines relaxed their grip on me. I rolled away and clambered to my feet where I wobbled unsteadily.

I looked down at my feet. They were encased in glass slippers. 'So when you *said* Cinderella spell you really *meant* Cinderella spell?'

'Ahuh,' Grams was grinning. 'Oh Izzy you look beautiful.'

I staggered to the mirror in the lounge and gasped at my reflection. I had on a crystal-encrusted, white gown. It sparkled with my every move. The gown had a V-neck with little cap sleeves, and was cinched at the waist before it flowed to the ground. My hair had been piled on top of my head and laced with more crystals. The pumpkin had even done my make-up.

I reached down and tried to tug a slipper off my foot. It was stuck tight.

'Not till midnight,' Grams said, chuckling.

'What do I do now?' I asked her.

'Well you probably should take the pumpkin and rodents outside and let them do their stuff.'

I picked up the pumpkin and carried it out to the driveway. The rodents scampered after me, making shrill cries of excitement. I placed the pumpkin on the ground and Scruffy stretched out his nose and sniffed it. He lifted a leg over it and the pumpkin reached a vine up and slapped him on the bottom. Scruffy bared his teeth, growling as the pumpkin lifted two vines like little fists, ready for a fight.

'Scruffy,' I said, laughing, 'leave him alone.'

He growled one more time and then sat beside the road and started to sniff his balls. Grams nodded her head at Scruffy and said, 'Do you want me to look after him tonight?'

'I don't know.'

The pumpkin settled the matter by throwing out a couple of vines and entangling Scruffy. They wrestled for a minute; Scruffy barked and growled as the pumpkin encased him. When he was finally freed, he was wearing a tiny tuxedo jacket, complete with bowtie.

'Guess not,' I said.

'Nice job on the outfits,' Grams said to the pumpkin.

It jumped up and down on the spot and then began to expand.

'Oh look, I've made his head swell,' Grams said.

As the pumpkin grew larger, several vines sprang to the side, looping around and around to form wheels. A door appeared on the body of the vegetable and a little seat up top. Then the whole pumpkin glistened and turned translucent.

I tapped on the side of it. 'Wow, it's glass.'

'Can I hop inside?' Grams asked. In response the door opened and Grams clambered up into the carriage. 'The seat's a bit hard,' she said, standing back up. A purple cushion appeared on the bench in the back. 'Much better,' she said, testing it out. 'Can't have your bottom going to sleep during the ride.'

The ludicrousness of the situation hit me and I started to giggle. I was going to hop into that pumpkin and go to the ball, dressed up like a princess. I turned to look at the rat and mice. 'Are you going like that?' I asked.

Squeaking, they ran in front of the carriage. Sparkles appeared in the air and floated down over them, touching them before settling to the earth. The rodents danced and twirled, getting bigger and bigger, turning faster and faster, until they were whirls of colour slowly morphing before our eyes.

When the dust finally settled, six white horses pranced in front of the carriage, and one man, with a suspiciously rat-like nose, wore a red, velvet suit and a large hat with a feather. He hooked the horses up to the carriage and then held the door open for me.

Scruffy let out a big huff and jumped up and lay on the purple cushion. He wasn't very happy about his tuxedo.

'Here goes nothing,' I said to Grams as I climbed on board and took a seat next to him.

'Have fun.' She waved at me through the translucent wall.

'Everybody's going to be able to see me.'

'I think that's the idea,' she said.

The coach driver flicked his whip in the air and we were off at a stately trot through the streets of Eynsford. He took the long way, obviously keen to make the most of the spell, and I had to sit and wave to the villagers as we passed by. It's not every day that a rat gets to wear a magnificent hat and drive a horse and carriage so I let him have his moment.

Eventually we came to Eynsford Castle. A large gap had been opened between the veils and was being maintained by a group of faeries.

We swept through the gateway. One minute we were in Eynsford, England, and the next we were in Isilvitania. The landscape stayed the same but that's where the similarities ended.

Garden faeries, flitting through massive oak trees, lit the way down the road. The air was sweeter and more wholesome, the trees taller and more numerous. But by far the biggest difference was the castle. It dwarfed our crumbling ruin both in size and magnificence.

The walls of the castle were swathed in lengths of silk and bathed in different coloured lights. Garden faeries congregated in the manicured trees, bobbing and glowing as they weaved an intricate dance. The fountains flowed freely, their water adding a magical tinkling to the music emanating from the castle. A full moon blazed overhead, bathing the whole scene in a silvery light.

The coach continued past the drop-off point at the front, and around to the back of the castle. I wasn't sure if that were a good or a bad thing as I still didn't know who had cast the Cinderella spell.

I gathered Scruffy into my arms as the coachman helped me alight from the carriage. He pointed to a pathway.

'You want me to go down there?' I asked him.

He nodded his head in affirmation and then climbed back up to wait for me.

Placing Scruffy down beside me, I approached the start of the path. The castle blocked the moonlight, and the way was dark and narrow. I wished I had a weapon. I wished I had a weapon but I didn't, so my glass stilettos were going to have to suffice. I moved slowly down the path, stopping to listen and allow my eyes to adjust to the dark. I could feel Scruffy pressed up against the back of my legs.

Just when I thought my heart was going to beat its way out of my chest, the path opened up to a courtyard. Light from the castle showed a huge fountain raining in the middle. Soft grass surrounded it.

A man, facing away from me, stood in the shadow of the fountain. He wore a resplendent, green coat that fell almost to his knees. Embroidery covered every square inch of it. His hands were behind his back and I couldn't see any obvious weapons, so I cleared my throat.

Aethan looked like a dark angel as he turned to face me. He sucked in a breath and stared at my face. 'I knew you'd look beautiful.'

Damn the man and his ability to make me blush. '*You* did this to me?'

He nodded his head. 'It was the only way I could think of getting you here.'

'You could have invited me.'

'You wouldn't have come.' He was probably right.

'Why did you want me here?'

'I need to tell you something.' He walked towards me, taking my hands and turning me so the light from the castle shone onto my face.

'What?' I was having trouble breathing. With him this close, alone, looking so dashing in his fine coat, I couldn't help but think of that kiss.

'I'm sorry I embarrassed you. I didn't think it through properly. I forgot you can't remember.'

Disappointment flooded me. So that was it? He wanted to apologise?

'It's not your fault I couldn't see the funny side of it.' I tried to pull my hands from his but he tightened his grip. The tinkling of the fountain drowned out any noise from the castle.

'You mean couldn't see the *irony.'*

'The irony?' Great Dark Sky he was handsome. Suddenly, I was glad he held my hands tight. I wanted to touch his face so badly I wasn't sure I would have been able to stop myself.

'Rako said we could ruin your memories if we told you anything. I would die before I did that.' He let go of my hands and stepped away, spinning so his back was to me. 'But I can't risk losing you.' His voice choked and he turned towards me, reclaiming my hands with his. 'No, I can't risk that.'

The look in his eyes became tender as he pulled me towards him. 'I promised I wouldn't,' he whispered, 'but I can't resist you any longer.'

The world spun as he moved even closer, bending his head towards mine. He traced the side of my face with his fingers as he stared into my eyes. 'I've missed you so much.' His body felt hard as he pressed me to him.

My breath caught in my throat and my knees felt weak. Was this *really* happening? Was I *really* getting what I'd been too scared to admit I'd wanted?

I closed my eyes and parted my lips, needing to feel his mouth moving over mine. Needing to feel the heat of his breath, the tease of his tongue… and *that* was when they attacked. A score of huge, dark-skinned warriors leapt from the top of the courtyard walls and surrounded us.

'Goblins,' Aethan hissed through his teeth, pulling me around so I was behind him.

I was welded into that dress and those shoes with no weapon. If I could ever have conceived of such a ridiculous notion, it would have been my worst nightmare come true.

Scruffy let out a long, low growl.

'Hide,' I said to him.

He whimpered.

'Hide.' I said it with enough force that his ears and tail went down, but he obeyed me, scurrying to a nearby hedge and diving underneath.

Aethan reached out to pluck a sword from where he had stuck it tip down into the grass. I turned so we were back-to-back. The least I could do was *try* to defend him.

Somehow I didn't think my stilettos were going to cut it. I wished fervently for a sword. I wasn't going to make it out of this alive without one. Hell, I probably wouldn't make it out alive even with one, but a chance would be good.

The air shivered in front of me and a sword fell into my outstretched hands. Did ***I*** do that? My magic was so random I couldn't be sure.

Goblin warriors were still jumping over the stone wall. They formed up, but kept their distance. I reached down and hacked at my skirt with the sword while I wondered what they were waiting for.

'Well, well, well, what have we here?'

Ahhh, of course. They had been waiting for Galanta.

Dressed head to foot in her garb of leather and bones, she seemed well recovered from the injury I had given her. Scruffy growled from under the hedge as she jumped down into the courtyard and paced towards us.

'Aethan, Isadora,' she said, nodding her head.

'Galanta.' Aethan's voice was terse with anger. 'What are you doing here?'

'I've come to take you,' she said. 'And to deal with *you.'* She nodded her head at me as she said the last bit.

One of his arms wrapped protectively back around me. 'Don't you think you've hurt her enough?'

'Hurt her? I haven't even begun hurting her.' She threw her head back and her evil laugh echoed around the courtyard.

'Now, now, Galanta,' Aethan said in a pleasant voice, 'you don't want to harm us.'

'I may not want to harm *you,'* she said, 'but I'd like to cut out your girlfriend's heart and have it for breakfast.'

I pasted a huge smile on my face and turned to face her. 'Eat shit and die.'

Aethan tightened his grip on me and placed himself back between us as she hissed and took a step towards me.

'You'll be smiling on the other side of your mouth when I'm finished with you,' she said.

'You mean face,' I said. 'It's smiling on the other side of your face.'

She roared with rage and pounced towards me. Scruffy barked in fury, darting out from under the hedge to bite her ankle. She looked down at him, in his little tuxedo, and snarled in disgust, shaking her foot to dislodge him.

I screamed in rage as she stabbed towards him, sweeping my blade to deflect hers. Power bloomed inside me, and without even thinking about what I did, I caught him up in a shield, formed it into a bubble, and cast him up into the air beyond her reach. He floated above us, barking and growling, but safe.

Aethan swung us around so that she was fighting him, not me. She tried to get through his guard to me, but he fought like a demon. I had time before her warriors attacked to admire his speed and grace. After that I was kept busy dodging and blocking as they tried to dismember me.

We put up a pretty good fight, standing back-to-back. Galanta, breathing heavily and clutching the side I had wounded, stepped back and signalled more warriors to attack us. I willed a second sword and fought double-handed, pulling on my magic to lend me strength. I took a slash to the arm and stabbed the warrior in the eye. He staggered to the side, leaving room for two more to attack.

Laughing like a crazy woman I engaged them. I could feel the adrenaline pumping through my veins. They may have been big, but they were slow and clumsy, relying on their brute strength to dominate. Sweat and blood soon speckled their bodies.

But as fast as they fell, others filled the gaps. Fatigue became our enemy. Just when I was beginning to despair, a cry of alarm sounded from above in the tower.

Galanta swore in fury, put two fingers into her mouth and whistled. At the noise, another score of warriors appeared on top of the wall. They jumped down and rushed us with no thought to their own protection. The sheer weight and size of them bore us to the ground, and even though we managed to take a couple out on the way, they easily overwhelmed us.

I felt my swords ripped from my grasp as I punched and kicked. The faeries' cries were getting closer, but shutting my eyes, waiting to feel the sting of cold steel, I knew they would be too late.

Then suddenly the goblins were gone. The first of the faeries charged into the courtyard and raced to the wall after them. I pulled myself into a seated position and turned to see if Aethan were all right. Terror shuddered down my spine as I realised he was gone.

'They've taken him,' I yelled, pointing over the wall.

'Taken who?' one of them asked me.

'Prince Aethan,' I said.

One of the faeries turned to another and issued a command. The smaller, slighter faery sprung nimbly over the wall and disappeared into the night.

'Izzy?' I turned to the sound of Wilfred's voice.

'Oh thank the Great Dark Sky,' I said as I stood up. 'The goblins have taken Aethan.'

'Have you hit your head?' Wilfred asked, looking me up and down.

I was in quite a state with my ripped skirt, my tousled hair, and blood soaked into the bodice of the dress (the pumpkin was *not* going to be happy), but I had to make them see the urgency of the situation.

'No,' I said, panic clawing at my insides. 'Galanta has kidnapped Aethan.' Tears welled in my eyes as the words came out of my mouth.

But Izzy,' Wilfred said, a confused look on his face, 'Aethan is at the ball, dancing with all the pretty girls.'

Chapter Fifteen

I Didn't See That One Coming

'Dancing with all the pretty girls indeed,' I fumed as we trekked through the castle to the ball. Scruffy floated in his bubble behind me, attached by a string of air. I wasn't ready to let him down till I knew he was totally safe.

I looked awful but I didn't care. After what I had just been through, I couldn't believe that Aethan was inside dancing. Perhaps I *had* tripped and knocked my head.

The ballroom was filled with brightly-dressed, young women, all waiting for their turn to dance with the Prince. It was a farce on the highest level. I didn't know him that well, but I was pretty sure Aethan would never have been a party to this disgraceful meat market. But sure enough, there he was, cradling a blonde in his arms as he waltzed around the dance floor. I heard a growl come out of my throat.

'That's not Aethan,' I said to Wilfred.

'I've been with him the whole night.'

'Would Aethan really put himself on display like this?'

'He did seem a bit excited by the whole thing.'

I pointed at the imposter. 'That's because that isn't him. Oh come on, we don't have time to waste.'

I waded through the women towards the floor. Some of them started to protest, but when they saw me, with blood tattooed on my face, they backed away in fright.

'Aethan Gabrielle,' I yelled from the edge of the dance floor.

The dancing stopped and everybody turned to look at me.

'Get her out of here,' Queen Eloise shrieked from her throne.

'Not so fast cousin,' I said. 'Aethan has been kidnapped by Galanta.'

'You're crazy,' she said. 'You can't handle the fact that Aethan doesn't want you any more.'

I strode over to fake Aethan and his simpering blonde. She pouted her lips and leaned in close to him. I managed to control my urge to scratch out her eyes.

'Now,' I said to the imposter, 'you and I both know you aren't Aethan. The real Aethan has just been kidnapped by goblins and I need you to stop this so we can save him.'

A look of horror crossed Aethan's face. 'That was never supposed to happen,' he said. And then slowly his features began to morph. His face melted and his body shrank and finally, all that was left was a small being who clung to my skirts and sobbed, 'You have to save him.'

'It's a pixie,' Wilfred said. 'Danoo?'

'Yes, friend of my master,' the pixie said.

'It's Aethan's personal servant,' Wilfred explained to me.

I watched as Danoo used the remnants of my dress to wipe his eyes. 'That's enough,' I said as he started to blow his nose.

Her shriek warned me just in time. Queen Eloise grabbed my hair and pulled it as she beat ineffectively at my head.

'It's your fault,' she screamed.

'How is this my fault?' I resisted the urge to kick her in the shins with my shiny, glass shoes.

Danoo jumped up and down trying to pull her off me, but in the end I was rescued from her feeble attack by a ruggedly handsome faery. I recognised him from the night he had fought goblins in his bed clothes.

'Cousin,' he said, 'you bring serious news. Can this be true?'

'King Arwyn.' I dropped to one knee. 'We have to save him.'

'We will child, but we need to prepare ourselves rather than run blindly into their trap.'

Even though every cell in me was screaming to go straight after them, what he said made total sense. Everything I had read on the craft of war told me he was right.

'A tracker has been sent,' Wilfred said.

'Excellent. We will prepare while we wait for his report.'

It took less time than I had feared for the faeries to arm themselves and prepare light backpacks with food and other necessary provisions.

'Here.' Wilfred handed me one of the backpacks and then took another look at my outfit. 'Aren't you coming?'

'Of course I am.'

'Why don't you borrow some clothes from one of the Fae women?'

I sucked some air into my cheeks. 'The thing is,' I grimaced, 'Aethan cast a Cinderella spell on me. I'm afraid I'm stuck like this till midnight.'

I had to give him credit for at least *trying* to keep a straight face. A small smile appeared at the corners of his mouth. 'What happens at midnight?'

'I'm not sure.'

His grin got bigger. 'But the dress?'

'Will go.'

'And?' He started to chuckle.

'Hopefully I will be left wearing what I had on before.' I was going to be royally pissed if I ended up naked.

'Are you going to be able to ride like that?' he asked.

'Give me your dagger.'

He pulled it out of its sheath and handed it to me, watching as I placed a split in each side of the skirt.

'Why don't you put these on?' I hadn't heard Isla approach. She held a pair of leather pants in her hands.

Trying not to catch the sharp points of the stilettos in the material, I stepped carefully into them. I shimmied them up under my skirt and fastened them. For a second they fit perfectly, then they disappeared from view, reappearing in a pile at my feet. *Stupid Cinderella Spell.*

'Shame,' she said as she bent to scoop them up. 'Your butt looked great in them.'

Wilfred let out a chuckle as she stalked away. 'Where's your sword?'

'Goblins stole it.'

He handed me a belt with a knife sheath attached to it. I held my breath as I placed it around my waist. Unlike the pants, it stayed where it was. He nodded his head in satisfaction and then handed me a long dagger.

'Why do I get the girlie knife?' I pointed at the long sword he had belted to his waist.

'You're the one wearing the skirt.'

The rest of the Border Guard was already mounted. I was less than thrilled to note Isgranelda amongst their ranks. She grinned when she saw me and whispered in Brad's ear. He let out a roar of laughter.

Rako sat at the head of the group. He gave me a long look but didn't say anything about my attire.

Scruffy whined from behind my head. 'Sorry boy,' I said. Once my adrenaline had abated, I'd not been able to control my powers. In the heat of the battle I'd only had to think of something and it was done. Now though, I was like a kid in a grenade store; you never knew what I might accidentally blow up.

King Arwyn and Queen Eloise were arguing up the front in quiet voices, but I could hear the words - she, little witch, not going near my son, and his choice - so I figured I was the source of the argument. When they had finally finished, King Arwyn told us all to mount up. I guessed he had won and I was going with them.

I took the reins of a mare from one of the Fae and climbed awkwardly onto her back. A horn blew and then suddenly we were off, racing as a group away from the castle. The moon's light was so bright I could easily see the terrain.

We travelled for a couple of hours over hills and through country that were both familiar and different to me at the same time. We passed farms with single-dwelling establishments, but there were no cities or villages. Eventually we approached a dark mountain standing like a lone sentinel on the plain. We slowed and then stopped.

I, for one, was glad to stop moving. It was all very well to decree I was going to save Aethan, but I was beginning to think that jumping into a saddle in the remnants of my glittery ball gown had not been such a good idea. My thighs felt rubbed raw.

'My kingdom for a sturdy pair of pants,' I muttered.

A small bubble finally appeared and floated towards King Arwyn. He stood still as the bubble popped on his face and then he turned to address us.

'The goblins have taken Aethan up Black Mountain.' He dismounted and the rest of us followed his example.

Wary of attack, we moved slowly towards the foot of the mountain where a small path started. I could see it winding its way treacherously up the spur. Two at a time we started the climb, slowing when the path narrowed to single file. I wasn't the only one searching the side of the mountains for goblins. If they decided to drop rocks on us we were in trouble.

My back was aching, and my calves screaming by the time we reached a clearing we could all fit into. I saw the tracker talking to King Arwyn and pointing up the next path.

A few of the Fae ran lightly up the path. They were shaking their heads when they returned.

'What's happening?' I asked Wilfred.

'I'm not sure.' He made his way to the front of the group and returned a few moments later. 'There's a barrier up ahead. We need to breach it before we can go any further.'

Frustration welled in me as the faeries tried to break the barrier. Aethan was somewhere on the other side and we had to get there before they killed him. I moved up to the front and turned my head from side-to-side. The barrier was invisible. I walked towards it with my arms outstretched, waiting for the tips of my fingers to meet resistance. There was nothing there.

'Well,' King Arwyn said, a few seconds later, 'can you pull me through?'

We linked wrists and I pulled him towards me until suddenly it was like pulling on a tree. I tugged harder. He winced and let go to rub his knuckles on his chest plate.

'That would be a no,' he said. His voice was neutral, but his face showed bitter disappointment. 'One at a time, try the barrier.'

I stood on the other side and waited while one-by-one the rest of the group pressed against the invisible force.

'Whizbang,' Wilfred muttered as he bounced off it.

The rest of them had no success either until Isgranelda walked up to it. She stood for a second as if something prevented her, and then she stepped through. Smiling like a cat in a house full of mice she stood next to me.

'I guess it's just the two of us,' I said.

'Try not to get in my way.'

'Get in *your* way? *You* try not to get in *mine*.' Oh yeah, this was going to be a *real* hoot.

'Teamwork ladies.' Rako clapped his hands together before we got to the hair pulling. 'Scout out the area. Find Aethan. You are not to engage the enemy. We *will* find a way through this thing.'

They would eventually, I was sure of that. The question was, would it be in time?

'You can't go dressed like that,' King Arwyn said, pointing at my ripped and bloodied dress. One of my glass heels had smashed off on the way up the mountain.

'What time is it?' I asked.

'Twenty minutes till tomorrow,' he said.

Oh goody. I was going to transform very soon and it was going to be in front of a horde of goblins. I wondered if they'd ever seen a naked witch.

'We have to go, and we have to go *now,*' I said. They might be planning some horrible ceremony for Aethan at midnight.

We travelled slowly up the path with Scruffy floating in the air behind me. I wondered what Isgranelda's familiar was. I'd never seen it. Maybe she didn't have one. Maybe she was half-human. She was *definitely* all bitch.

The path we followed twisted and turned through the mountain till I lost all sense of direction. It had remained the same width as we climbed, but suddenly it narrowed. Isgranelda turned so her back was against the rock and slid her feet sideways as she edged carefully along the rocky ledge.

Halfway across, I made the mistake of looking down. It was so narrow I could see the drop off through the tips of my glass slippers. I froze, staring at the valley below. It was so far away. If my foot slipped an inch I was going to find out exactly how far it was. A cold sweat broke out on my body.

'Don't look down,' Isgranelda growled.

I ripped my eyes away from it and stared straight ahead while I panted. If *she* could do it, ***I*** could. I pressed my hands against the wall behind me, looking for finger holds as I slithered sideways until the path widened again.

We travelled for a few more minutes before Scruffy let out a low growl.

'Shut him up,' Isgranelda muttered as she squatted to peer around the next corner.

'Shhhh,' I said to him, squatting as well.

Isgranelda pulled back from the corner and moved closer to me. She held up five fingers. Then three and pointed to herself, and two and pointed to me.

'Why do you get three?' I hissed.

Ignoring me, she drew her sword and launched herself around the corner. I yanked the dagger from my belt and scrambled to catch up.

I rounded the corner to see her kick a goblin off the length of her sword and twirl to attack another. So much for not engaging the enemy.

I leapt into the air, pulling my legs into a tuck as I somersaulted over a goblin. I landed behind him and dragged my blade across his throat. Hot blood gushed onto my hand as he fell.

Scruffy barked and I ducked, feeling the air above my head move as a sword swept through the space where my neck had been. I spun and kicked up with my glass stiletto. My attacker let out a bellow of pain as the heel embedded itself into the soft tissue of his groin. I heard a ripping sound as my leg whipped back down.

Blood darkened the front of his pants. He clutched at his privates and I swung my blade up under his ribs and into his heart. He was dead before he hit the dirt.

Isgranelda had already disposed of her three, a small smile on her face. I felt a moment of chagrin as I wiped my blade off on the material of my skirt. *Smug bitch.*

The path continued around the side of the mountain until it reached a clearing. The moon shone onto a large, flat rock in the centre. Aethan lay unmoving on top of it. Was he alive? I couldn't tell from where I was standing.

I had expected a hoard of goblins would be guarding him, but there were none. That in itself stunk of a trap, so I resisted the urge to rush to his side.

Isgranelda wasn't so concerned. She stalked to the middle of the clearing and swung her sword from side-to-side.

'What are you doing?' I whispered.

'You still have no idea do you?' She started to laugh, a low guttural sound. It sent chills down my spine.

Scruffy barked and it took me a panicked moment to realise he wasn't barking at goblins. He was barking at her.

She stretched slowly, as if luxuriating in the feel of her muscles, and then she started to change. Her hair grew longer, changing from blonde to black as it matted into dreadlocks. Her outfit shifted until leather, covered with small bones, encased her. Her nails lengthened and thickened till they were black talons.

Oh buzznuckle. This *so* was not good.

Her eyes became black with the eerie-red circle I remembered so well. She threw back her head in a triumphant laugh as she finished her transformation.

'Surprise,' she said, grinning at me with her pointy teeth.

I couldn't believe it. All this time? All this time Isgranelda had been Galanta? It made no sense at all.

'So, is this when I get to kill you?' My voice sounded braver than I felt. The memory of her melting her knife into my skin still haunted me.

'This is when you get to try.'

Scruffy's barks became vicious as he snarled and leapt at her with snapping jaws. Suddenly, he was gone from the bubble. He appeared beside my feet, hair bristling out of the top of his tuxedo as he bared his teeth and growled.

He attacked, latching onto her ankle with his sharp little teeth. She snarled and swung back her foot, shaking it from side-to-side. He flew off, letting out a yowl as he smacked into a rock. I ran towards him but he pushed himself up, shook his head a couple of times, and launched himself at her again.

This time she lifted her arm and stabbed down towards him with the tip of her sword.

'No,' I shrieked. Rage roared through me as I raced towards them. I threw out my hands and her sword smacked into an invisible barrier an inch from his back. I wrapped him back up in his bubble and tossed him into the air.

'Not my dog, you *bitch.*' I threw myself at her.

Stuff this stabbing people thing; I wanted to feel my fists pounding into her flesh.

Darting inside the reach of her sword, I palmed her in the face, slamming her head back. Before she could recover I twisted her sword arm until her weapon fell from her fingers. Then I balled my hand and smacked her in the head as hard as I could. Blood flew as her nose snapped to the side.

I followed it up with a flurry of fists; pummelling into her with all my might.

Torture me? Try to kill my dog?

I growled as I smacked her. The feel of my fists beating her flesh satisfied my urge to hurt her.

'Instimo,' she gasped as I grabbed her hair with one hand. I lifted my other arm to punch her but it was like moving through molasses. Slower and slower my arm went until I couldn't move it at all.

'Ha,' she said, and she punched me in the gut.

If I could have, I would have bowed over with the pain. As it was I fought against my invisible bonds as she punched me again and again. I choked in air, struggling to breathe around my burning chest.

She stopped and straightened her crooked nose. Pushing it back into place she wiped away the blood on the back of her arm. Then she picked up her sword and waved it in front of me. 'This ends *now.*'

I grappled with her spell, desperately feeling along the edges of it with my mind. There. I could feel the join where she had melded the air around me. I flowed into it, stretching it and pushing it until finally, it fell away. Screeching, I dived to the side as her sword swept through where I had been standing.

I spat some blood out of my mouth and pulled Wilfred's dagger out of the holster. Holding it high I faced off against her.

'Just like a witch to bring a knife to a sword fight.' She waved her sword at me.

'It's knife to a gun fight, stupid.'

She snarled as we circled each other. I risked a quick peep at Aethan. Was his chest moving? I couldn't be sure.

She launched the first attack. Letting out a blood-curdling scream she drove the tip of her sword right at my chest. I ducked to the side, and her thrust carried her past me. I kicked out, managing to hook one of her feet. She tripped and staggered towards where Aethan lay. As if he weren't there, she swung back to face me.

Why *hadn't* she killed him? What was she waiting for?

I moved around the area, staying on the balls of my feet to minimise the instability caused by the broken glass slipper. She looked down at my feet and burst out laughing. 'Why are you wearing those?'

'Glass slippers?' I asked as if it were the most normal thing in the world. 'You should try some. They're very comfortable.'

'They don't look very robust.' She flicked her blade down and pointed at the broken heel.

'I broke that off in one of your warrior's chests,' I said. 'Such a shame. These were my favourite.'

She spat in my direction. 'Think you're so clever,' she sneered. 'You don't realise I've got you in a double bind.'

I had no idea what she was talking about. That made me nervous.

'No matter what you do tonight you will lose.' She laughed like it was the funniest thing ever.

I couldn't see how that could be true. Either I lost and she killed me, or I won and killed her.

'You must choose between him,' she flicked her head in Aethan's direction, 'or yourself.'

Double bind, him or me? I hated cryptic sentences.

'Shut up and fight.' I threw myself at her, slashing the air with my dagger. She darted away and I leapt into the air to land behind her. She twirled faster than should be possible, bringing her sword up to block my thrust. I kicked her in the chest, and forced her back.

As I swung and slashed, parried and blocked, the strangest feeling crept over me. Tingling. Starting at my head and working its way down my body. I ignored it as long as I could but then it changed to prickles.

'What are you doing to me?' She raked her arms with her nails.

'Nothing.' I gritted my teeth as invisible ants crawled over me. Scruffy whined as he scratched and nipped at himself.

'Stop it.' Galanta hopped up and down on the spot, slapping herself with the palms of her hands.

'I'm not doing it.' I jiggled side-to-side trying to rid myself of the sensation. Pins and needles prickled my whole body. Scruffy spun around and around, trying to bite his tail.

She tore her nails through her dreadlocks, scratching as if she had a bad case of nits. Her talons had left long welts down her arms. Blood trickled from a couple of them.

As suddenly as it had come on me it was gone. Instead of my torn ball dress I wore the outfit I'd had on that afternoon. I glanced up at Scruffy who was naked except for his black, studded collar. He was contentedly licking his balls.

Galanta ran in circles, slapping at her body as if she were on fire. She collapsed on the ground, writhing like a serpent. 'Make it stop,' she begged.

I almost felt sorry for her, but then I remembered her burning me and all feelings of pity went out of my head. I knew I should finish her off while she was down, but I couldn't. Not in cold blood. If the situations were reversed I had no doubt she would have, but I wasn't her. I wasn't a monster.

A shimmering light glowed over her, encasing her from head to foot. She screamed again and again, spasming in time with her shrieks. And then finally, the screaming stopped, the shimmering vanished, and she lay there, dressed in a white, crystal gown and glass slippers.

I couldn't help myself, I burst out laughing.

'What have you done to me?' If I'd thought she'd been mad before, she was in a total rage now.

'I didn't do anything.' I stepped back as she climbed unsteadily to her feet. 'It's a spell that was cast on me. It seems to have stuck itself to you.'

She looked down at the gown with a disgusted look on her face. 'How long will it last?'

'I'm only guessing,' I warned her, 'but probably till midnight tomorrow night.'

She took a step towards me, wobbling on the high heels. Snarling, she tried to yank them off.

'They won't come off till then.' I was trying to memorise every detail so I could share it with Aethan when he woke up. 'If it's any consolation,' I said, 'you look lovely.'

'I don't look lovely,' she yelled. 'I look *hideous.*'

'Oh well, that's just *my* opinion. Why don't you go and ask your warriors?'

At the mention of them, her face took on a look of horror. 'I can't allow them to see me like this,' she said. And then she turned and sprinted towards the edge of the cliff. I watched as she propelled herself off the side, and then rushed to watch her rapid descent to the ravine below.

She disappeared long before she reached the bottom. One minute she was falling, and the next she was gone.

I rushed to Aethan, kneeling beside him to check for a pulse. It was there beneath my fingertips. I breathed a sigh of relief. I wasn't too late.

I called him and shook him, and, when that didn't work, I slapped his face. But nothing that I did could wake him. Galanta's words on the double bind entered my head but I pushed them aside. I refused to be blinded by her callous words.

What should I do? I couldn't carry him all the way back, and I didn't want to leave him in case a goblin showed up.

I reached up and pushed his hair back from his face. It felt as soft as it looked. I traced a finger over the top of one pointed ear, and then, feeling voyeuristic, I did what I had wanted to since the first time I'd seen him. I ran my hands through his hair.

My hands brushed the rock under his head and sharp edgings caught at my fingertips. Gently, I lifted his head. Words were etched into the stone. I shuffled him sideways across the stone so I could read them.

Only blood can let me live,
Only blood can set me free.
Blood of my own one true love,
Or of a descendant born of me.

Huh? Did the poem have anything to do with the spell on Aethan?

I pondered the words. It was obviously a call for blood but I was pretty sure I didn't satisfy the rules.

He was a distant cousin though. Did that count?

I poised the tip of the dagger over my wrist, gasping as the sharp blade penetrated the soft skin. Blood welled to the surface and I turned my arm so that the first drips landed on the words inscribed in the stone. They sizzled as they landed.

My blood pooled on the rock, boiling and bubbling. Then it sank, disappearing into the stone until it was gone. There was not even a stain to show it had been there.

I heard the tremor before I felt it. From deep within the earth, the rumble worked its way to the surface where it ruptured the rock, cleaving it into two pieces.

Aethan and I were tossed to the side. He landed on top of me, the weight of his body forcing me down. Cold air flowed from the fracture. It wound around me, caressing me with its icy touch. It chilled me to the core of my heart and sent a shiver of fear down my spine. And then, just when I was wondering what I had done, Aethan opened his beautiful eyes and looked straight into mine.

I heard a click deep inside and my two halves flowed together. My memories meshed into one perfect whole. I felt things, I saw things, I knew things I hadn't known before. But somehow it was as if I had always known.

Like two decks of cards being spliced together, the memories flicked into order.

I knew Aethan. I *knew* him. With every cell in my body, every fibre of my core. We had hunted, we had fought, we had laughed, we had loved.

The irony he had tried to tell me about? In our hearts, and our minds, we were already betrothed. I was bonded to him and him to me.

I laughed as I reached for him, crushing his lips to mine. It had been too long since I'd held him. Too long since I'd tasted him. I breathed him in as our lips moved and our tongues touched. I needed more of him, always more of him.

I pushed my hands up under his shirt and ran them over the glory of his body. So hard, so strong, so mine.

He broke the kiss, leaning back so his weight was off me.

'I remember,' I said. 'All of it.'

He cleared his throat and tilted his head to the side. 'This is all very nice,' he said, giving me the cheeky grin I loved so much. 'But… do I know you?'

He was joking. He *had* to be joking.

'Where are we?' He pushed himself up and held a hand out to help me. 'The last thing I remember is fighting goblins.'

A double bind. She'd said she had me in a double bind.

'With me,' I said. 'You were fighting them with me.'

He shook his head. 'I left the ball to get some fresh air. They came over the wall and surrounded me. I was alone.'

Air left my lungs and I sagged back onto the broken stone. She'd said I would choose between him and me.

Tears slid from my eyes. He didn't remember me. I ached to hold him but his eyes beheld a stranger.

I had found him and lost him in the space of a heartbeat.

'Why are you crying?' His perfect face held only concern.

'Ummm. I'm happy you're alive,' I said, wiping my arm across my eyes. 'We'd better get out of here. The others will be worried.'

'Ahhh,' he peered over my shoulder, 'why is there a dog floating behind you?'

'Scruffy is my familiar.'

'You're a witch?'

'Half,' I said.

Great Dark Sky, he didn't remember me.

'I hate to have to ask this,' his embarrassment was palpable, 'but I don't know your name.'

I tried not to cry but traitorous tears leaked down my face. 'It's Izzy.' I could feel my heart ripping into a million pieces. 'Isadora.'

'Well Isadora, which way do we go?'

He *never* called me Isadora.

'That way.' I pointed towards the head of the path, turning away so he couldn't see my face.

Gone. All gone.

The ache in my chest threatened to crush my lungs. I tried to suck in air, but it wouldn't come. Bright lights danced before my eyes as my knees buckled.

'Are you okay?' He shook my shoulder gently.

'Aethan.' The shout came from the pathway. A few seconds later a contingent of the Border Guard rounded the corner. They spread out over the open space, their weapons drawn.

'I thought I'd lost you son.' King Arwyn pulled Aethan into a rough embrace.

Wilfred reached a hand out to me and pulled me back to my feet. They had been bare when the Cinderella spell had struck and now sharp stones dug into them.

'Oh Willy,' I cried, throwing myself into his arms.

Is this how he had felt when I hadn't remembered him? Like his heart was being ripped from his chest?

Wilfred pulled away and peered down into my face. 'You remember.' It was a statement not a question.

I nodded my head.

'So, why the tears?'

Aethan pointed a finger between Wilfred and me. 'So… you and Isabella?'

'It's Isadora.' I managed to correct him without a fresh sheet of tears.

'What? No.' Wilfred pushed me away. 'You know she's like a sister to me.'

'How would I know that? I've never met her before.'

A stunned silence filled the clearing. Everyone there, except King Arwyn, had been aware of the relationship between Aethan and me.

Rako cleared his throat and broke the silence. 'Ahhh, where's Isgranelda?'

'Gone,' I said.

Before I could elaborate, a drum boomed. A few seconds later another one reverberated throughout the mountains. Then a third.

'Raiding parties,' Rako said.

'And he's not speaking about the sort of party that includes balloons and a gift bag,' Wilfred said.

The more drums that joined in, the more the hair on the back of my neck stood on end.

Rako snorted. 'If these guys give you a gift bag it will probably contain one of your body parts. Time to go.'

I followed the rest of the Guard as quickly as I could. But while they ran I trotted my way through the sharp rocks.

'Keep up,' Rako called over his shoulder.

Hmmmphf. Easy for him to say.

It wasn't long before they were out of sight.

'This is just great,' I said to Scruffy as the noise of the drums got closer. 'I save his arse and then he runs off and leaves me to get killed.'

I paused at the start of the narrow ledge. 'Don't look down,' I told myself. I tried to concentrate on that thought, and not the fact that as well as the drums I could now hear guttural cries coming from further up the path.

How far away were they?

Scruffy growled from the safety of his shield balloon.

'I know, I know,' I said, clearing the ledge and picking up my pace. I rounded a corner and ran into Aethan and Wilfred.

'They're coming,' I said, hobbling past them.

'She's got no shoes on,' Aethan said, picking me up and throwing me over his shoulder. 'Why has she got no shoes on?'

I growled and Wilfred let out a laugh. 'Kind of your fault dude.'

'How is this *my* fault?'

I bounced up and down on his shoulder, the damage from Galanta's punches making me want to yelp. But we were making much better time like that than with me limping, so I shut my mouth on my curses. Instead I lifted my head and peered up the path the way we had come.

The moon's rays touched this side of the range and I could see the path winding up through the mountains. It was crowded with goblins, pushing and shoving as they ran. An arrow clattered to the ground about ten feet behind us.

'You might want to run faster,' I shouted.

Another arrow raised a cloud of dust. This one was closer.

'Leave me.' I struggled to get down. Aethan was far too important to die saving me.

Wilfred spun and fitted an arrow to his bow. Within the space of a few seconds he launched three arrows at the goblins in the lead. Two of them dropped to the ground, and the ones behind stumbled over them. More goblins ploughed into them and, like a caterpillar, the effect made its way up the mountain. From sprint to standstill, the line of goblins swelled in breadth and I saw several bodies plummet off the side of the mountain.

We rounded a corner and I looked ahead under Aethan's arm. Rako and a couple of the other Guard stood at the end of the path. 'Hurry,' Rako called, as if Aethan wasn't sprinting as fast as he could. 'Is she hurt?'

'Only my pride.'

The rest of the Guard was already mounted. Aethan ran towards the horses. Placing me back on the ground, he climbed onto the back of the mare and reached down to pull me up behind him.

I ducked low and threw my arms around his waist as the roar of the goblins indicated they had cleared the mountain path. An arrow nicked my leg, ripping the denim of my jeans. I saw a second one bounce off the back of Wilfred's armour as he leaned low over the neck of his horse.

I wished I were wearing armour. I wished it with all my might. Armour, a sword and a pair of boots. I closed my eyes and concentrated on it. And when I opened them I still had no armour, no sword and bare feet.

Stupid unreliable powers. What was the point? They were more likely to get me killed than not.

The sound of the goblins faded away behind us, and our group dropped from a gallop to a canter, and then to a trot.

'Don't want to tire out the horses,' Aethan said over his shoulder.

The fact that he felt the need to explain that meant he still had no idea who I was.

I sucked in a big breath of air and pushed the pain down. We would fix this. He would remember me again. He would. I had to hang onto that belief. And in the meantime, I had to do what he had done for me. Say nothing.

The sun was just peeping over the trees when we got back to the castle. I was exhausted from a combination of the night's activities and the strain of the awkward silence between Aethan and me.

'Get some sleep,' Rako ordered. 'We will debrief at sixteen hundred hours.' He jumped nimbly from the black stallion he had been riding and strode over to me. 'That includes you.'

Ignoring Aethan's hand, I slid off the back of the mare. It hurt for him to touch me so dispassionately. I nodded my head and limped off to where I had left the coach.

A pumpkin lay discarded on the ground, but the rat and mice were nowhere to be seen. I picked the pumpkin up. It didn't seem right to leave it there to rot in the sun. I hugged it to my chest as I contemplated how I was going to get home.

'Guess we're going to walk, boy,' I said to Scruffy. I concentrated hard, trying to dissolve his air shield, but he continued to float just beyond reach. I was going to have to get help.

He ruffed and then slowly faded until he disappeared from the bubble, reappearing a moment later at my feet. I gave him a steely stare as he trotted to the nearest bush and squatted.

'Get in.'

I turned to see Wilfred leaning out the window of a bright-red sports car. The dash was covered with shag-pile carpet, and fluffy dice hung from the rear-view mirror.

'Like you're not hairy enough.' I opened the passenger door and climbed in, falling backwards into the bucket seat with a groan. It felt so good to be almost lying down. Scruffy jumped onto my lap and then into the back of the car where he stretched out on the back seat.

Wilfred put the car into gear and headed for the break in the veil. 'Where's your familiar?' I asked.

'Don't have one.'

'But you're not full-faery and I doubt you're half-human.'

'I told you, my Mumma was an orc.'

'I thought you were joking,' I said with a laugh. Why had I never known that about him? There was *so* much fodder there for jokes.

'You don't get this hairy any other way.' He scratched at the orange hair puffing up from under his collar. 'So are you going to tell me what happened up there?' He slowed a little as we drove between the lines of faeries holding the veil spell. They looked as exhausted as I felt.

I sighed and picked at a partly broken nail. 'Isgranelda turned out to be Galanta. We fought. She left. Then I woke Aethan.'

He looked over at me. 'You speak like a man.'

'That's because you trained me.' I had spent almost as much time with the big man as I had with Aethan. I sighed again. 'I'm trying to pretend it didn't happen.'

He laughed as he pulled up in front of my house. 'You act like one too. All right, I'll wait till the debrief.'

I opened the door and Scruffy jumped back onto my lap and down to the lawn. He barked and ran towards the front door, probably off to beg Mum for food.

Wilfred reached over and put a hand on my shoulder. 'This will sort itself out, just you wait and see.'

'I hope so,' I said as I climbed out of the car. 'I really hope so.'

Chapter Sixteen

Impending Doom

Grams, Mum and Sabby were waiting for me when I came in the front door.

'By the Great Dark Sky,' Sabby said as she threw herself at me, 'I freaked when you came into the ball covered in blood.'

'Most of it was goblins'.' I looked over at Mum and Grams.

'You're not going to stop doing this sort of thing are you?' Mum asked.

I shook my head. 'Sorry.' I hated worrying her.

'Why couldn't you be an accountant? Mary Simpson's daughter Lucy is an accountant. *She* never rocks up to balls covered in goblin blood.'

'Lucy Simpson is as boring as bat shit,' Grams said.

'True.' Mum hopped up to put the jug on and I knew I was at least partly forgiven.

'So,' Grams clapped her hands and leaned towards me, 'tell me everything. What happened when you got to the ball?'

Even though Mum seemed to be starting to accept my choice to be a Border Guard, I didn't want to push my luck. I also didn't want to talk about Aethan. 'I'm sorry,' I said, 'I need to get some sleep.' Grams' face fell. 'I promise I'll tell you,' I crossed my fingers behind my back, 'but not now.'

I needed food as well, but sleep was coming in at number one on my to-do list.

I showered long enough to remove any gore and then sank onto my mattress. Bright light slipped around my curtains, illuminating the room. 'Eric,' I said, 'I need to sleep.'

The room immediately darkened until I could just make out the shape of my own hand. 'Perfect,' I said. I reached up and pulled the dream-catcher off the head board. There were things I needed to do.

As soon as I shut my eyes I stepped into Trillania. Normally I would have concentrated on the thought of Aethan and gone to wherever he was.

I squished my eyes shut tight while I fought the urge to cry. Once I had it under control I concentrated on Emerald, sending out a mental cry to her.

Her voice responded sleepily in my head. *Safe,* she told me. *Well.* Sleepy images chased those thoughts: soaring towards the ground, talons reaching to pluck a fat sheep from a paddock; racing over a wind-whipped ocean; flying through clouds, the misty shapes coating her in a fine layer of mist; and I realised she was dreaming.

My thoughts turned to Galanta and the world around me shifted. Trees towered above me, shadowing me with their huge trunks. I tensed at the sound of drums beating. I hadn't had one good experience that involved goblins and drums.

Frozen with indecision, I paused. Did I go to see what the drums were about or did I try to find another Guard. Problem was that the Guards on duty now would be from the Southern Hemisphere, where it was night at the moment, and I didn't know any of them.

The drums increased in tempo. Whatever they were up to it was going to happen soon.

I shook my head and ignored the feeling of foreboding that was lodged in my throat with a scream. Then I crept through the forest, stopping to check around me as I went.

A large bonfire flickered through the trees. I slowed my progress, scurrying from trunk to trunk till I found a large, low thicket. I pushed my way into it until I could see out the other side.

Galanta stood naked in front of the fire. Sweat trickled between her breasts and down her stomach. She held a knife in each hand and her head was thrown back as she swayed and chanted.

The hairs on the back of my neck stood on end as her voice reached a fever pitch. The drums beat so fast they were a continuous thrum. Her voice grew louder and louder as she shrieked and screamed and then suddenly, instantly there was silence.

I had a bad feeling about whatever was about to happen.

She opened her eyes and stepped back from the flames as one of her warriors thrust out an arm. His hand was wrapped tight around the neck of a little girl.

Her eyes were wild with terror as she cried and suddenly, ***I*** was a little girl, hiding under my bed.

I bit down on my hand till the pain returned me to the present. I hadn't gone through everything I had to let *this* happen.

I started to push out of the thicket but Emerald's mind was suddenly in mine.

Stop.

I have to help her.

You will die.

I knew she was right, but at that point in time, with irrational fear burning inside me, I didn't care.

Her mind pressed down on me, preventing any movement.

Witness.

I didn't want to witness. I didn't want to see this. I didn't want to know.

Bright blood splashed as Galanta whipped a knife through the girl's neck. Her scream of pain and terror, and Galanta's screech of triumph, masked my whimper.

Galanta shook her, holding her so that the blood dribbled out of her neck and onto a stone.

A sick feeling started in the pit of my stomach. I recognised that stone. The two broken bits had been pieced back together, but it was the stone Aethan had been lying on when I'd found him.

Oh Great Dark Sky. Terror beat inside my stomach and ice formed in my veins.

Steam started to rise off the stone as blood ran freely over it. The little girl's head hung. Her eyes were closed, but her chest still moved as her heart pumped her blood from her body.

That icy breeze that had escaped the breaking stone - what had it been?

The cloud of steam grew larger, as it pulsed in the air. It warped and waned and, as the blood flow continued, it took on the form of a man. I heard Emerald hiss in my mind.

Oh Sky, what had I done? What had I *done*?

The shape shifted its smoky limbs as if stretching.

Galanta laid the girl's head on the stone and picked up her legs. The more blood that flowed, the more solid the man became.

My heart thundered in my chest as I stared at him. Dread owned me. Its icy fingers held me down. Panic swelled and roared in my ears.

I could hear Emerald chanting in my mind. *It's him. It's him.*

Her terror amplified my own. Spreading its wings inside me till madness fluttered frantically at the edges of my mind.

Just when I thought I couldn't take any more, just when I thought I would start screaming hysterically, it was done.

Galanta tossed the dead girl to the side and opened her arms as the man stepped away from the stone. Hard, lean muscle dressed his naked form.

She bowed low and her warriors prostrated themselves.

'You have done well Galanta.' His voice had a sonorous quality.

Oh please don't let it be him.

'Thank you my Lord,' she said.

He spun on the spot with his arms held wide and then he started to chuckle. 'It feels good to be back,' he said as he laughed.

Chills ran down my spine and Emerald whimpered in my mind.

He lifted Galanta's head with a finger until her eyes met his own. 'I will make them pay.' His voice was cold and hard.

'Yes my Lord.'

'I will hunt them down and crush every last one of them.' Insanity danced through his words. 'Nobody, and I mean *nobody,* gets away with tricking me.' He threw both arms in the air and a bolt of lightning arced across the sky. 'Nobody gets away with tricking Santanas Gabrielle.'

It was him, it was him.

Great Dark Sky save our souls.

Santanas, the War Faery, was back.

THE END

About Me

Hi there, I'm Donna Joy Usher. I started writing my first novel when I was seven. With no idea about plot or character development (I mean I was only seven) my storyline quickly disintegrated into a muddled jumble of boring dialogue between two horses.

Disillusioned, I gave up writing stories for quite a while after that. Instead, I concentrated on my studies, eventually graduating as a dentist.

After many years of 'drilling and filling' I turned to writing in an effort to escape the seriousness of my day job. During that time I created my first book, The Seven Steps to Closure, and discovered that I love nothing more than making other people laugh. Well that, and my two miniature schnauzers, Chloe and Ebony.

I currently live near the Swan River in the beautiful city of Perth. When I am not working or writing, I love to kayak, ride my bicycle, and sip chai lattes at the local cafe.

You can connect with me on Facebook (@authordonnajoyusher), Goodreads, Instagram (@donnajoyusher_theauthor), and my website donnajoyusher-theauthor.com

What to Read Next

Faery Forged

Book Two in The War Faery Trilogy

Galanta is only one step away from successfully releasing Santanas. The faeries must either stop her or hope that their allies stand strong in the coming storm. While they seek her out, they are forced to cement old allegiances and create new ones. With this in mind, Orion offers himself as a groom to the treacherous night faeries, asking only that Aethan go in his stead to choose his bride. Meanwhile, Galanta's spell means that while Izzy now remembers Aethan, he has no memory of her.

As Aethan, Izzy and Wilfred travel to the realm of the night faeries to bring home Orion's bride, they are pursued by goblins and hunted by giants. To make matters worse, Santanas' strengthening power means that terrifying monsters are unleashed against them. They will need all their strength and cunning to make it safely home and to stop Galanta from releasing a mad War Faery upon the world.

Follow this link to find out where you can buy *Faery Forged*: https://donnajoyusher-theauthor.com/get-faery-forged/

The *War Faery Trilogy* is available in eBook, Print or Audible formats.

Faery Revenge

Book Three in
The War Faery Trilogy

The veil is sealed for thirty days and Izzy is looking for distractions to help her forget about Aethan. When a strange dragon and rider appear in Eynsford, Izzy and Isla travel with Emerald to another world. There, they discover the mystical city of Millenia; home to a band of renegade dark faeries, Ubanty and dragons.

Unable to return, Izzy is forced to battle pirates, assassins, and the advances of the devastatingly hand- some Turos.

But at home, the shadow of war is marching across the land. Santanas is back and gathering an army, and Izzy is needed.

Follow this link to find out where you can buy *Faery Revenge*: https://donnajoyusher-theauthor.com/get-faery-revenge/

The *War Faery Trilogy* is available in eBook, Print or Audible formats.

Agents of APE

Book One in

The Alien Private Eye Series

Meet Siccy. She's an arse-kicking, smart-mouthed chick from the Aussie outback. She likes her men complex and her life simple, but all that is about to change. You see Siccy's just woken up from a nap to find that five years have passed.

Now, her fiancé's shacked up with her best friend, and strange creatures are trying to kill her. And if all that wasn't weird enough, the darkly, mysterious Elliot arrives, determined to recruit her as an Alien Private Eye.

But is Elliot who he says he is, and are his claims that the planet is in danger true? Siccy must put her broken heart aside if she is to decipher the truth, thwart the attempts on her life, and go on to save the world.

Visit https://donnajoyusher-theauthor.com/get-ape/ to view purchasing options.

Cocoa and Chanel

Book One in The Chanel Series

Faced with the unattractive options of an affair with her boss's husband or the unknown, Chanel Smith chooses the unknown and unwittingly traps herself into joining the New South Wales' Police Force.

More interested in fashion than felony, she staggers through training and finds herself posted to the forces most notorious crime hot spot, King's Cross. There, she becomes entangled in a case of the worst kind - a serial killer targeting young women.

As she is drawn further into the seedy underground in her attempt to unravel the truth, Chanel makes new friends, new enemies and attracts the attention of the killer. Can she solve the case in time, or will she become the killer's next victim?

Visit https://donnajoyusher-theauthor.com/get-cocoa/ to view purchasing options.

The Seven Steps to Closure

Winner of the 2012 elit Publishing Award Humor Category.
Finalist in the 2012 Shirley You Jest Book Awards.
Finalist in the 2013 Indie Excellence Awards Chicklit Category.
Honorable Mention in the 2014 London Book Festival.

Tara Babcock awakes the morn- ing after her 30th birthday with a hangover that could kill an elephant - and the knowledge she is still no closer to achieving closure on her marriage breakup.

Things go from bad to worse when she discovers that, not only is her ex-husband engaged to her cousin - Tash, the woman he left her for - but that Jake is also running for Lord Mayor of Sydney.

Desperate to leave the destructive relationship behind and with nothing to lose, she decides- with encouragement from her three best friends - to follow the dubious advice from a magazine article, *Closure in Seven Easy Steps*.

The Seven Steps to Closure follows Tara on her sometimes disastrous – always hilarious – path to achieve the seemingly impossible.

Follow this link to find out where you can purchase *The Seven Steps to Closure*: https://donnajoyusher-theauthor.com/get-7steps/

Made in the USA
Las Vegas, NV
06 February 2023